About the Storyweaver series . . .

These true stories will not only open your children's eyes to how God is defending orphans around the world, but will also show how he provides for them today through the obedience of Christ's disciples, young and old.

—Rick Carter, HGBC Missions Coordinator, Northern KY

I love this book because it has true stories about real kids who need families and love and don't have what most kids do.

—Chelsie Voge, age ten

My son and I read *Tales of the Not Forgotten* together, and it really challenged us in the way we think about our world. It encouraged us to talk about poverty, suffering, the call of the gospel, and our response to the Great Commission. I'm so thankful for the discussion times he and I had as a result of reading this book together.

—Matt Markins, D6 Conference Cofounder

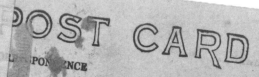

POST CARD

CORRESPONDENCE

I read *Tales of the Not Forgotten* on a flight and tried not to make a scene as I constantly fought back the tears. . . . Since then, any time I'm in a conversation about helping kids develop a heart that breaks for what breaks our Lord's heart, this book is the first thing I mention.

—Tina Houser, Publications Director, KidzMatter, Inc.

Beth captures not only the harsh realities of life for children all over the world, but also how they intersect with beautiful stories of God using his people to live out the gospel—all written in a voice ideal for preteen kids. These stories have much potential for mobilizing this generation to make a difference in the world.

—*Jenny Funderburke, Minister to Children,*
West Bradenton Baptist Church

Tales of the Not Forgotten is a masterfully woven book. Beth in her patented story-telling style connects you to the cry of the orphan throughout the world. . . . My daughter now understands better what it mean to "look after orphans and widows."

—*Curtis Cecil, father of six, two adopted*

Beth is one of the most anointed ministers of the gospel I know. Her powerful storytelling leaves you—and your preteens—feeling emboldened to take part in how God is moving in the world.

—*Evan Doyle, Communication Specialist,*
KidzMatter, Inc.

One of the highlights of my year was getting to know Beth and to get to see and hear her heart for God and his kids around the world. I'm excited about this new book and how God is defending the orphan. Make sure you read *Tales of the Not Forgotten*—it's a game changer!

—*Jim Wideman, children's ministry pioneer,*
Jim Wideman Ministries

This book changed my daughter's life—she was brought to tears reading the stories of the children. Her teacher stated that she can tell this book changed Ceili.

—*Chelle Lynn, reader*

I was truly captivated by *Tales of the Not Forgotten*. Beth places the reader right there beside the characters as they go through their pain and turmoil, and eventually experience the touch of our great Lord's hand. This book tugs at your heart, prompts you to do more, and demonstrates that God will never leave us, nor forsake us (Hebrews 13:5).

—*Amy Tuell, Mission Team Leader*

This book has provided a graspable path for my children to be exposed to the needs of kids around the globe. Together we praise God for what he is doing and ask, how can we help?
— *Krista Regan, mama of two boys who love Jesus*

The Storyweaver series reminds us all that nothing happens by accident. These stories are living proof that every act of kindness is part of God's master plan. They inspire us to look twice, extend a hand, offer a smile—you never know when the Storyweaver will use us to change others' lives, or use them to change ours.
— *Tina Rogal, sponsor mom of kids in Mexico and Africa*

The Storyweaver series helped me to see that the face of Jesus is a child I have never met, in a place I may never go to, hurting in a way I may never be able to fully understand. . . . These stories show just how far the arm of the Lord reaches and just how deep and wide his love is.
— *Melissa Parsons, wife, mother, and servant*

Tales of the Not Forgotten is a must read because it highlights the desperate plight of the orphan around the world through gripping, true stories. 163,000,000 orphans get a voice in this work.
— *James Wendell Bush, Minister to Students, Rosemont Baptist Church*

Beth is a master storyteller—one of the best there is anywhere in the contemporary church—to which any of the tens-of-thousands who have heard her speak can attest. As cohost of our national radio show, *Real Life, Real Talk*, *I have the joy of hearing these stories every week. . . . In Tales of the Not Forgotten* she transports readers through her personal and heartfelt style into the gripping stories that mark Back2Back's labor of love among orphans and impoverished people around the world. Once I read *Tales* I invariably found myself talking to everyone I knew about the God-sized, compassionate, riveting, and profound stories I found inside.
— *Dr. Rob Hall, Research Analyst, Cincinnati Hills Christian Academy*

Throughout Scripture we see that God's heart is for the orphans. . . . In a compelling way, Beth moves the open-hearted person from just caring *about* the orphan to becoming a person who will care *for* the orphan. She presents the clear and emotive reality of life as an orphan in such a manner that people rise up to take action for these precious ones.

—*Steve Biondo, SVP, Family Christian Stores,*
President, The James Fund

Beth Guckenberger and her husband Todd have a gift for sharing God's love with the fatherless and the forgotten. . . . They have truly delighted themselves in the Lord and he has given them the desires of their heart. What an example set for us to imitate in our own lives.

—*J.D. Gibbs, president of Joe Gibbs Racing*

Tales of the Not Forgotten has been a great book for our family to read together. We're hearing the stories and being inspired as a family to care more for orphans.

—*Matt Massey, Lead Pastor at Northstar*

After reading these stories, it's difficult to see the world as "out there" instead of "next door" and impossible *not* to want to help more children like these. . . . The Leader's Guide is absolutely perfect—it contains everything you would need to turn this book into a series of mission lessons for kids. . . . It's truly perfect for young youth groups, homeschool groups, Sunday school classes, etc. I read many great books, and some stick in my head for a long time afterwards. Some I'm eager to share with my friends and family . . . but never before have I had plans to share a book with so many others within days of turning the last page. As you read this book, you can't help but want to be a part of someone else's story—to have a hand in helping them see that the God of the Universe has not forgotten them.

—*Amy Bradsher, wife and homeschooling mom,*
anestintherocks.blogspot.com

TALES OF THE DEFENDED ONES

TALES OF THE DEFENDED ONES

BETH GUCKENBERGER

WARNING: THESE STORIES MAY CHANGE THE WAY YOU SEE THE WORLD

Standard®
PUBLISHING

www.standardpub.com

Published by Standard Publishing, Cincinnati, Ohio
www.standardpub.com

These stories are inspired by true events and real people. In some cases, names
were changed to protect identities and details of dialogue and actions were
imagined. Six billion stories are unfolding daily. These are just a few.

Also available: *Tales of the Defended Ones Leader's Guide*, 978-0-7847-3698-2;
Tales of the Not Forgotten, 978-0-7847-3528-2; *Tales of the Not Forgotten
Leader's Guide*, 978-0-7847-3527-5.

Printed in: United States of America
Acquisitions editor: Dale Reeves
Project editor: Laura Derico
Cover design and illustration: Scott Ryan
Interior design: Dina Sorn, Ahaa Design

All Scripture quotations, unless otherwise indicated, are taken from the *HOLY
BIBLE, NEW INTERNATIONAL VERSION*®. *NIV*®. Copyright © 1973, 1978, 1984,
2011 by Biblica, Inc.™ Used by permission. All rights reserved worldwide.
Scripture quotations marked (*NLT*) *are taken from the Holy Bible, New Living
Translation*, copyright © 1996, 2004, 2007 by Tyndale House Foundation. Used
by permission of Tyndale House Publishers, Inc., Carol Stream, Illinois 60188.
All rights reserved. Scripture quotations marked (*The Message*) are taken from
The Message. Copyright © by Eugene H. Peterson 1993, 1994, 1995, 1996, 2000,
2001, 2002. Used by permission of NavPress Publishing Group.

ISBN 978-0-7847-3697-5

Library of Congress Cataloging-in-Publication Data

Guckenberger, Beth, 1972-
  Tales of the defended ones / Beth Guckenberger.
    pages cm
  Summary: A collection of fictionalized stories based on the real lives of five
children in Ethiopia, Mexico, the United States, and Cambodia as they intersect
with Christian missionaries who seek to help them as they were called by God, the
Storyweaver, to do. Includes facts about each country and the issues faced there.
  ISBN 978-0-7847-3697-5 (perfect bound)
  [1. Christian life--Fiction. 2. Missionaries--Fiction. 3. Orphans--Fiction.] I. Title.
  PZ7.G93463Tad 2013
  [Fic]--dc23
                          2012039111

18 17 16 15 14 13   1 2 3 4 5 6 7 8 9

To my fellow Back2Back Ministries
staff members, our extended family,
and to those with whom we partner,
there is not a day that goes by that
I don't say thank you to the Lord
for co-laboring with you.

INTRODUCTION
THE DEFENDER

Their Defender is strong.

—Proverbs 23:11

There are millions of stories out there, billions really, because everyone has one. You have a story and so do I.

My story started in Indiana and then went to Ohio, and now is taking place in Mexico. It began with two brothers, lots of bike rides, and regular servings of ice cream. Today, there are new characters in my story; there is a new setting and plenty of plot twists.

We are all layers of many story lines in our lives. You have a story as a brother or sister, a story as a neighbor, a story as someone's child, as an athlete, or as an artist. God made you a girl or a boy, the

Beth with two of her children, Emma and Evan.

firstborn, or maybe the middle child. He made you a morning person . . . or not! You might speak two languages, be a reader, or have some funny talent that makes others laugh. Whatever is true of you . . . it is part of your story.

God is the Storyweaver, and he's writing your story right now.

My name is Beth and today I live full-time in Mexico as a missionary, witnessing the stories of orphans I love very much. It's important that we not only care about our own stories, but also about the stories of others. Orphans don't have a lot of people watching their stories. It's our privilege to watch them and then tell about them, and sometimes even to be a part of them. That is a bit of the God-design he put in us, to care for others. He cares about each one of us and wants to bring us into each other's lives.

Who has God asked you to care about?

Proverbs 23:10, 11 says "Do not move an ancient boundary stone or encroach on the fields of the fatherless, for their Defender is strong; he will take up their case against you." God is the great Storyweaver, and he is also the great Defender.

God defends us all in a million different ways, but this book you now hold is about watching for ways God is fulfilling his promise in defending "the fatherless"—children who, for one reason or another, lose the support and protection of their birth parents. I will share with you a story about two boys adopted from Ethiopia, about an orphaned boy with special needs who lives in Mexico, about a young girl who found herself in the U.S. foster care system, and about a girl slave from Cambodia. All of them needed a Defender.

There are parts of these stories which might be hard to read. You might feel bad for the people in the stories, or sad about the things they had to suffer. At some point while reading this book, you might even ask, "I have heard other horrible stories of children hurting; why didn't God defend them? And why did any of these kids have to suffer at all?"

That's a very important question to ask. And it's a question you might find yourself asking over and over again, even when you become an adult.

It can be confusing, but before we worry that God is not really doing his job, let's watch and learn how he *does* work. Through asking good questions and working to find the answers, we can learn and grow and find out things about God we hadn't seen before.

God is the Defender of all, and he can defeat any evil. I am completely, 100 percent convinced of this truth. But because we live in a world that is broken and hurting, and is filled with broken and hurting people, sometimes very bad things happen. When those bad things happen, and not every ending feels like it turns out happy, we have a choice.

We can look around and see the bad things and think we have seen it all . . . and decide that God is not in it. Or, we can look around and know that we are seeing only a part of the story—a teeny, tiny, minuscule part. It may be a very important and difficult part, but it's still only a part.

God is the Storyweaver, and he knows exactly what is happening, to everyone, everywhere—and for every why, he holds the answer. You can see in these stories how many times he had already set into motion the answer to the question the child would later ask, or the solution to the need the child would encounter.

was eventually placed in charge of the whole land of Egypt. When a severe famine came on that land, everyone came to Joseph for help—even those brothers who had sold him and let their father believe he was dead.

When Joseph finally revealed himself to his brothers, he did not hurt them. He didn't even yell at them. Instead, he gave them the best land in the country and took care of them. And he said to his brothers, "You intended to harm me, but God intended it for good to accomplish what is now being done, the saving of many lives" (Genesis 50:20). Joseph knew God the Storyweaver was his Defender.

We have to train our ears to listen for messages of hope and train our eyes to look for God's hand. The stories in this book are good practice for that. (The stories in the Bible are great for that too!) We also have to train ourselves to look around us and ask, "What is my part in this story? What can I do?"

Let's get started. And as we go, remember . . .
the story's not over yet!

Chapter 1
BEN AND JOSEPH'S PATH

My hand out all day and nothing to show for it . . . again. Adina sighed and looked at her bundle—the baby boy swaddled in the cloth she had just untied and let down from her back. He was still sleeping, even after how hard he'd hit the ground when her weary arms had faltered, and she'd let him down too quickly. She knew he was weak, but she hoped the milk she still had to give him would sustain him . . . at least until she figured something else out.

She rubbed her eyes. *Tired. I am so tired these days.* She squinted through the dusky light down the dirt road at a cluster of mud-and-straw houses in the distance, a typical sight there on the outskirts of Soddo, the southern Ethiopian town they called home. She spoke out loud, though no one was around to hear, except for the sleeping baby and a few wandering goats. "*Ab*, I know you see us. Will you

ETHIOPIA

show me, one more time, where
we can find shelter tonight?
Where can we sleep tonight?" She
finished her prayer by thanking
God for another day. "This one was
harder than yesterday. Please wake me
in the morning with new mercies, Lord."
After resting for a while, she lifted her precious
bundle to her back again and trudged down the road.
She found a metal roof to settle under, and there the
two dozed off and on, all night. It was not her metal
roof, and she did not know the owner. But she wasn't
the only one borrowing it for the night—a sure sign
that the home was either abandoned or the owner

POST CARD

CORRESPONDENCE

Amharic is the second most-spoken Semitic language in the world, after Arabic, and the official
language of the Federal Democratic Republic of
Ethiopia. Amharic writing looks a lot like Arabic
writing. The Amharic words in this story will be
written so you know what they would sound like.

Ab means "Father God."

just didn't care. She slept only in bits, painfully aware of the blood she kept coughing up in her sleep. Her mouth tasted salty and bitter,

The faithful love of the LORD never ends!
His mercies never cease.
Great is his faithfulness;
his mercies begin afresh each morning.
—Lamentations 3:22, 23 (NLT)

but she had no water. The baby boy stirred with his mother's movements, but did not wake. He was used to the sound of her coughing and the feel of her arms around him.

It was cool in Soddo at that time of year. Sleeping outside was uncomfortable. Yet Adina often found herself waking up in the night with her clothing wet with sweat. She didn't understand this, or why her chest and back ached so much. She blamed it all on the weather. *That must be why I'm struggling so much in the day—I can't find peace in the night. I can't breathe this cool air.*

Adina had some friends, but no family. She saw the same women every day on the same corner, buying and selling what they could find to make enough for some *injera*. Friendship was hard to find in the streets, but Adina had one friend she trusted. Gabra was an older woman, and Adina liked to spend hours talking to her as they sat on the street corner together. They told stories about their childhood, stories about the men in their lives, stories about the future they imagined might one day appear.

It was Gabra who found Adina early one morning, passed out from pain. Eventually, they learned that Adina had tuberculosis, a disease that would kill her. There was no good story to be told anymore about her future.

She was dying, and facing it now was the only way she could save her son.

For a while Gabra carried the bundle on her back, so Adina could rest as often as possible. But soon Adina had no more milk and any work became virtually impossible. Her fevers and dizzy spells became more frequent. Sometimes whole days would pass without Adina's knowledge, while Gabra took care of her and the boy too.

POST CARD

CORRESPONDENCE

Injera is a pancake-like bread that is used to scoop up spicy dishes, such as **doro wat** (chicken stew) and **mesir wat** (lentil stew).

Tuberculosis (TB) is an infection transmitted by breathing in or swallowing the bacteria called tubercle bacilli. It usually affects the lungs, causing fever, coughing, and difficulty breathing. Treatment is especially hard on people who already have poor health and nutrition. Because treatment in Ethiopia is difficult and expensive to get, many people go without medicine. In 2007, Ethiopia had more than 314,000 cases of TB.

She and Gabra had passed by the church many times in the last month. They didn't speak of it, but when the day came, they both knew it. It was time.

Adina had been planning for this since the moment she heard the doctor tell her she had tuberculosis. She knew there was simply no other option. Still, dozens of times in the last few weeks, as she'd walked the street along the orphanage's entrance, her heart had cried out to her Father in Heaven. *Is this your answer? Is this what I am to do? Do I have to let go now?*

How many times had she looked through the

doorway at the children inside and watched the kind of women who went in and out? *Will they have enough for my son? Will they care for him? Oh God, oh God, oh God . . .* She stayed at a place Gabra had found for them that was close by the church, and Adina often sat up in the night, rocking back and forth with pain—both the pain in her body and the pain in her heart. Sometimes the thought of what was coming was more than she could bear.

But now the day had come. She waited that morning until Gabra had gone to find work, not wanting to ask any more of her. But she didn't even know

Soddo Christian Hospital has been serving one of the most populated and impoverished areas in Ethiopia since 2005. They seek to supply severely needed quality health care in a compassionate and sacrificing manner, treating each patient with respect. (More information can be found at www.soddo.org/home.asp.)

if she could take one more step with her child on her back. She couldn't remember the last time they had eaten. *Was it a day ago? Two?*

Somehow she made it to the door of the orphanage. "Listen to me, please!" she grabbed the arm of a woman at the door. "I am sick, very sick, otherwise I wouldn't . . . I couldn't do this." Her voice, hoarse from coughing, trailed off. The woman at the door waited patiently, holding Adina up with her arm. Adina mustered the energy and courage to raise her eyes to the woman's gaze. "Look at me! I want you to give my son a family—a good, Christian family. I want you to make sure they know and love Jesus. Do you hear me?" Her words shook with emotion and

Ethiopia is one of the oldest countries in the world, and Christianity has been a large part of its culture since ancient times. The Ethiopian language is full of references to God.

her thin fingers dug into the woman's arm. "Can you promise me that?"

By this time, others had joined them in the doorway and helped the woman usher Adina into a waiting room. The workers tried to comfort her, assuring her they'd look for a family that shared her faith. They explained some papers to Adina and helped her fill them out. Tears spilled down her face as she told them her son's name, "Abenezer." She signed with her thumbprint, had her picture taken, and then walked away.

No more bundle on her back.

Adina left the orphanage that afternoon with a mixture of peace and pain in her heart—and a few days later her heart stopped altogether.

Born twenty-five years earlier than the baby in the bundle was a girl with a heart for all children and a curiosity about the world around her. As a small child she whispered to her mother, "One day I want to see Africa."

The first prayers went up.

Future adoptive parents, Keith and Shelley, at their wedding.

The workers at the orphanage unwound the baby bundle and found a very, very malnourished boy. His body was tiny, and his head was large. They didn't know what was wrong, but the women were certain something was.

For nine months, the baby lived in that orphanage, waiting for a family to see his picture and respond, waiting for governments to agree on conditions and approve his ability to be adopted. During that season, the baby never spoke and never walked. His actual age and physical condition remained a mystery.

The girl eventually met a boy with a heart for Jesus and a love for children, and a year after they married in front of God and family, God saw fit to give them twin boys.

Their family had begun.

The family grew with another baby, and now there were three children under three in the busy house. The tug of the girl's heart that started in childhood grew as well. Now a grown woman, she became drawn to international ministry, and together these young parents—living smack in the middle of the United States—began to look at the world outside their walls.

And what did they see? They saw orphans and poverty.

One night the couple stayed up late talking about these huge, overwhelming issues. "What can we do? How can we make a difference?" one said to the other.

"What about adoption?" The question hung out in the air for a moment. "Could God have a child out there, waiting for us?"

Listening, they heard in their prayers a whisper. *Ethiopia.*

Eventually, Abenezer's referral was accepted by someone in the U.S. The women in Soddo prepared the boy, who still preferred to be bundled up, to move to Ethiopia's capital city, Addis Ababa. There he would stay while the adoption proceedings went forward. As the women said good-bye to the boy, they prayed over him, thanking God for his new family and asking for angels to watch over him.

In the city, he was soon taken to see a doctor who examined him and had tests done to see what was wrong with the child's head and brain. The family who would adopt him had asked for more information on his condition so they could be prepared for his care.

Abenezer trembled on the cold examination

table and stared up at the bright lights. *Where is my blanket?*

Things seemed to move quickly for the family of five. They had seen on the waiting list a very young boy who was listed as hydrocephalic (meaning he had a condition where there was a build-up of fluid putting pressure on his brain). They found out no one else had inquired about this little boy.

They talked with doctors they knew in the U.S. and educated themselves on his condition. They imagined what it would look like to have a child who needed brain shunts and constant care. They prayed, cried, and asked God if this was truly what he wanted for their family. They were afraid of the unknown ahead of them but still felt led to move forward.

Yes.

"That one. We want him. Abenezer."

They asked for a scan to be done in Ethiopia, so they could learn the extent of the brain damage. But they promised their yes would still be yes, no matter what.

The adoptive mom was concerned about her baby boy being taken on such a long drive to the capital city—eight hours—but she was happy to hear he would be held the whole time. The twins, young as they were, began to pray for their new brother. They asked if he would be scared. Their mom assured them, "God hears our prayers and is moving even now to protect our little boy. He will be his Defender." This answer satisfied them, but they kept praying, again and again, for a boy they had only seen on the computer screen.

Then one day they got a call about the little boy's condition. Here is what the mom wrote that day in her blog:

> WOW.
>
> I don't really know what to say.
>
> For the past month, we have been preparing ourselves for a child who may need some extra attention, brain surgery, and maybe lifetime care from us.
>
> Today we received a phone call from our agency, along with a copy of the CT scan report AND HE IS FINE!!!!! I cannot believe it!!!! The exact wording from the medical sheet is:
>
> Conclusion: Normal Head CT.
>
> WOW. I don't know what God is up to, but I am once again feeling very blessed to be a part of it.

In Addis Ababa, the doctors shook their heads over Abenezer's scan results. He was much older than they had originally thought. He wasn't a tiny baby with a big head, he was a severely undernourished toddler with a small, developmentally delayed body.

A scene from Addis Ababa.

They sent the report on to the adoption agency, who sent it on to the parents, who praised God for this amazing news.

The baby bundle, or Ben, as he would soon be called, waited while paperwork was finished and filed, not knowing or understanding at all what God was working together on his behalf. He did not know that God had been working on a woman's heart for more than twenty-five years to shape her into his new mother. He did not know that somewhere far away two little boys were praying for their new brother.

Kassa with a picture of Ben.

He did not know that God had watched over his own birth mother to allow her to bring him to that orphanage in Soddo.

All he knew was he was glad to be where he was, where he was warm, and taken care of, and . . . never hungry.

God the Defender had provided for that too. Ben needed to gain weight. His body needed nutrients so he could begin to grow properly. So God found the perfect person to help this boy do just that—the orphanage cook.

Kassa came to love Ben very much, and every

morning she would tie Ben on her back in the same way his mother had done, and she would feed him over her shoulder all day long. She would give him tastes of soups and stews from big pots. For every batch of injera she made, she would fold a small one up and hand it to the boy to chew on. She gave him as much fruit and vegetables as she could get him to eat. And eat he did! Kassa was an answer to the prayers of the adoptive family, thousands of miles away.

The great Storyweaver was at work.

The adoptive parents were relieved to hear about their son's tests. They were glad he was healthier than they had hoped, and thankful his care would not be so difficult for him. But more than that, as they had been praying, their hearts had grown bigger still, and they had come to know something. They didn't want just one baby. They wanted two!

This family God was building—that would one day take vacations together and go to school together and fight with each other and love each other—now had three babies in the U.S., one bundled on the back of the orphanage cook, and one yet to be found . . .

Desta felt her swelling abdomen. *How am I going to do it alone?* Already with the one baby it was hard to gather and carry the ingredients home to make injera. Then to make enough not only for the woman she worked for in the apartment below, but also enough to sell in the market? She sighed and looked at her son, playing on the floor with a wooden spoon. *How many more years until he can help?* she wondered.

The summer months passed and her stomach grew harder and heavier every day. She could still hold her son and carry him, but she tried to prepare him for the change coming. "I need you to walk more; there will be another one in my arms soon." He didn't understand, but looked at her intently when she talked. "I don't know how we will do it, carrying the ingredients and the baby and you from the market and up the stairs every day."

She put him down on the floor again, and he tottered over to the pots he had been playing with. She sighed and rubbed her lower back, where a throbbing ache had started to bother her. She smiled weakly at the boy's faltering steps and remembered an old Ethiopian proverb: "Slowly, but surely, the egg will walk on its legs."

According to recent figures, about 39 percent of the Ethiopian population is living on less than $1.25 per day.

One morning, Desta recognized the hardening and softening rhythm of labor. The baby would be coming soon. She grabbed her son's hand and half-held him as they made their way down the stairs to her employer's home. She knocked on the door.

The woman opened the door and greeted her, "*Endemin nesh?*" But she immediately saw that Desta was not well. Desta breathed deeply as she handed over her son. "I will be back before nightfall." She pushed some food and clothing into the woman's hands. "Please, take him for the day. I will come back as soon as the baby arrives."

Reluctantly, the older woman received the squirming child. "OK, but just for today. I can't help you all this week. Mind you, I still want fresh bread by the weekend."

"Sure, OK, I understand," Desta panted, hunching over, then left quickly before the woman could change her mind. She made her way out of the city and to a clinic she had heard about—a safe place for women to give birth. She stopped every few steps and waited for the contractions to pass.

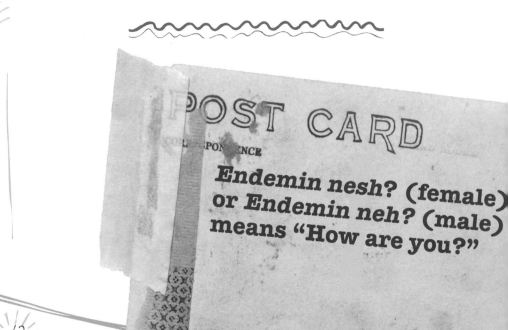

POST CARD

CORRESPONDENCE

Endemin nesh? (female) or Endemin neh? (male) means "How are you?"

Night had fallen, and the boy's mother still wasn't back. *I should have known*, the older woman huffed to herself. *Now how am I going to sleep with this little one kicking me all night on my mat?* He had been quiet most of the day, as if sensing he needed to behave. Although still a little young, he had just learned to walk, and he moved around the room efficiently. There wasn't much for him to harm, and truth be told, he was good company. *But not for long*, she thought. *I am too old for this! His mother needs to come back!* She settled down on the mat with the boy and tried to sleep.

By nightfall the next night, she knew something was wrong. It wasn't like Desta to not come back and not at least send word that there was a problem. She muttered, "I will do this for a few more days, but I can't go much longer. My body hurts most of the time—picking him up just makes the aching worse." The boy watched her as she spoke. He seemed to understand she was struggling and quietly curled up on the mat.

By the week's end, the woman had had enough. The boy wasn't letting her sleep, and he wasn't comforted easily anymore. "I don't have time for this! Or money! Or energy!" The boy looked up at her with wide-open eyes.

Father to the fatherless, defender of widows . . .
God places the lonely in families.

—Psalm 68:5, 6 (*NLT*)

She gathered up Desta's son and his few things and huffed and puffed her way to the orphanage in their village. "I don't know much about him—not his name, or even his age. He seems very smart, like he is aware of things in a way most babies aren't. His mother left to deliver another baby and hasn't come back in a week. I think she went to the Girium clinic, but I don't know for sure. If she ever comes back, I'll tell her the boy is here." With that, she handed over the little boy and walked away.

After a week or two of investigating, the orphanage learned the mother had died in childbirth, along with the baby girl she had been carrying. The mission that now housed her son paid for the woman to be buried in the common grave.

The average life expectancy for a woman in Ethiopia is about 58 years.

And the wonder boy—who looked around his world, seeming to take in everything—needed a new family.

The orphanage sent his paperwork to the capital, noting his eligibility for adoption. After a month or so, they received word he was to be brought to the capital city. All the way from Soddo to Addis Ababa, this wonder boy looked out the window (when he wasn't busy eating injera). He didn't know where he was going, and had never traveled so far, but it was OK—his Defender-Kinsman was leading the way.

As the girl with a heart for Africa waited with her pastor husband and their three babies to go to Ethiopia, they prepared for the baby bundle named Ben with the growing body to come home. Then another call came. A wonder boy with a tremendous appetite and a keen mind was waiting for a family as well—were they interested in yet another son?

The parents on this faith mission of love flew into Addis Ababa on a Monday night, wondering aloud to each other, "When will we see the boys? How will they react? Will we meet them at the same time? What will we name the second one?" Questions danced around their minds all night long. Finally they woke in the morning, ate their granola bars, and met the orphanage director in the lobby.

The director had both Ben and the other boy with him.

The man looked at the boy with no name and said, "I think he's a Joseph. Let's name him Joseph. Ben and Joseph." He practiced saying the names together.

The woman tilted her head and smiled at the boys. "Really?" she asked her husband, "I don't know . . . are you sure?"

"Yep. I'm sure. A boy separated from his family, but protected and then picked up by God. A man of destiny. That's Joseph."

"I don't care what we call him, let's just call him ours." And the mother held out her arms to her two new sons.

The children's home director watched them all together for about ten minutes and then left, giving them time alone as a family. These new parents and new sons and brothers had their first real moments of family together. Holding, looking, crying, touching, kissing, praying . . .

The boys looked at each other and at these two new grown-ups in their lives with curiosity. The man and woman gathered them up and took them to find something to eat. Very soon they found out that Joseph liked to eat everything, while Ben only wanted bread and bananas.

Ben stayed quiet and often hid his face—his

The parents and boys meet for the first time.

shyness overcoming him. But Joseph befriended every person he walked by—smiling at them and staring with his big eyes. One of the persons who walked by was a hotel worker, who wondered about this new family. She approached and asked the obvious questions of the parents. These were questions they would hear again and again, but the boys did not understand the answers at this time.

Joseph listened as the man and woman answered the questions—they seemed so excited. They said something to the hotel worker, and she said, "Really?" Then she leaned over to Joseph and spoke in Amharic, pointing to the man and woman, "These are your new parents! They are taking you home. Now this is *Abaye* and *Emaye*!"

Joseph, the wonder boy, repeated those names over and over—Dad and Mom. And Ben smiled shyly in his new mom's arms.

The celebration wasn't complete until the three siblings-in-waiting back in the U.S. could circle around their new brothers and say their names. Five days later, the mom and dad and two boys flew to South Bend, Indiana, and all of them found a new way to say and be "family."

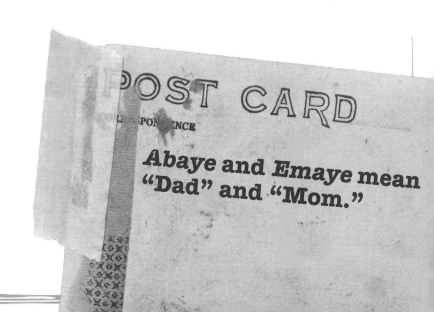

POST CARD

CORRESPONDENCE

Abaye and Emaye mean "Dad" and "Mom."

Family members brought Tommy, Hunter, and Anna to the airport. The children beat their new African instruments together and played—at first around each other and then, eventually, with each other.

This scene in the airport, of people crying over children, of shy smiles and small beginnings, would be repeated in church and at home and at the coming family gatherings. In each scene everyone could see the Storyweaver was at work.

It took faith, courage, obedience, a whispered call, three mothers, two governments, a lot of plane tickets and diapers and many prayers—but in the end, God, the Defender, rescued these two boys and gave them a family.

Ben and Joseph with their new siblings. Ben is second from the left; Joseph is fourth in line.

When Ben first came home to Indiana, he was the size of a young toddler. He could barely walk. He said only one word, and he knew no expressions. Now he is one of the tallest kids in his class and has the best laugh. He can throw a ball farther than his siblings and is one of the most likeable kids you could imagine.

Joe (Joseph) had a wild streak from day one. He is truly one of a kind. He can win a room over in a heartbeat. He is crazy smart and has won the hearts of many little girls in his school.

From Beth's Journal

This is how the Defender God wrote this chapter for Ben and Joseph! He picked them up and planted them elsewhere, not because he loved them more than others, not because where they were was bad, but because he in his sovereignty has written new story lines for them. Lines that involve Tommy, Hunter, and Anna. That involve grandparents and school and church and who knows what else? All I know is, I can't wait to read the next chapter.

REMEMBER THIS

In Ben and Joseph's story, there were many people praying for them long before their new family even met them! Those praying people are a key part of this story. I have been praying for a family of three little girls who are getting adopted this year and I know those prayers will affect their transition, their attachment with their parents, their hearts, language skills, and adjustment to their new home. Will you pray for kids being adopted right now? God knows their names and wants to involve you in their stories through prayer.

Both boys have the love of Jesus in their hearts and are learning every day to have compassion on the world around them—including the faraway parts of the world where they took their first breaths, and where so many are praying right now, in need of a Defender.

Sometimes it can be hard to know what to pray for or how to talk to God. Romans 8:26 (NLT) says that "the Holy Spirit helps us in our weakness. For example, we don't know what God wants us to pray for. But the Holy Spirit prays for us with groanings that cannot be expressed in words."

What do you think is difficult about praying? What are some things you've prayed about lately?

Write your thoughts about the story of Ben and Joseph here.

Chapter 2

ANTONIO'S GIFT

Young Christina tried to listen to the doctor, only half hearing him through her pain and exhaustion. "Your son experienced some trauma in delivery. Only time will tell if it caused damage to his brain. If something seems abnormal about his behavior, or if he appears to be having seizures, make sure to seek medical attention immediately."

Yeah, because it was so easy to come "seek medical attention" this time. Christina's eyes looked right past the doctor to the door, her thoughts spinning. *I have to get out of here.* She had been plotting how she could sneak out of the little Mexican clinic without paying the bill for her baby's delivery and care. It's not that she didn't *want* to pay, she just didn't have money to offer. She didn't have anything. Just this baby boy.

When the nurse left her alone for over an hour,

it seemed like a window of opportunity had opened for her. Hunched over her small bundle, she snuck out of the busy, crowded clinic. Once outside on the street, she flagged down a bus. She settled into a seat with a small groan, trying to find a comfortable position. Her body ached everywhere, as if she had been beaten all over. Then she looked down at the little face sleeping in her arms and for a moment, she was happy.

Only twenty-four hours later, her boy, Antonio, had a seizure for the first time. Christina was staying in her grandmother's house in Mazatlan, trying to make a go of it as a parent. She didn't know what was happening to her baby.

What had the doctor said?

It was *mucho miedo!*—she was scared! He looked very sick—his eyes rolled back in his head. Christina held him tightly in her arms while his tiny body shook.

She said a prayer to a God she knew was listening. She just didn't know if he knew their names.

As Antonio grew, he shook regularly. Sometimes Antonio's dad would come around with money and Christina would take her son to a doctor for medicines. These would work for a season, but the money came in spurts and could never be counted on. And the medicine was never really a perfect fit for Antonio.

When Antonio was four, he was sent back from his neighborhood preschool class with a note that said that "he is scaring the other children when he has seizures, and I'm sorry, but as the teacher to everyone, I don't feel equipped to handle Antonio's issues and don't have the time to focus on just one child. He is a

POST CARD

CORRESPONDENCE

Spanish is the primary language of people who live in Mexico and many Central and South American countries. Five hundred million people speak Spanish around the world.

Mucho miedo means "very scary."

lovely boy, but this school isn't the right fit for him."
Christina sighed. It was the only option she could
afford.

So that was the end of Antonio's experience in
school.

Antonio's father came in and out
of his life for a couple of years,
bringing gifts at Christmas
and money around Easter,
and whenever he came, he
would bring a small *piñata*
with him. Antonio loved
when a surprise would eventually fall out. Because Antonio
loved it so much, his father remembered to bring one
every time he came. One summer, when Antonio was
around six years old, Christina realized that his father
hadn't come around in a while. Their last conversa-
tion hadn't ended well. He didn't feel comfortable
around Antonio, and had asked questions Christina

couldn't answer. Whether it was that, or because he was involved with people Christina felt were dangerous, it didn't matter now. That was to be their last conversation.

The only good part about his dad being gone was that Antonio didn't seem to notice his absence.

Meanwhile, finding steady work was virtually impossible for Christina. No one could or would watch Antonio for her. Most days Christina would walk through the neighborhoods of her town, knocking on the gates of the bigger houses. Whenever anyone answered, she would ask if she could work for the day in exchange for food. Antonio would always trail behind her, content in a world where he knew his mom was nearby.

"Antonio, help me with these weeds." Christina came up with small jobs to keep him busy, and that plan usually worked. He would help until he was all sweaty, forgetting even to drink, focusing intently on the task at hand. More than once, his mom walked

A piñata is a colorful container, often made from papier-mâché, hung up as part of a celebration (such as a birthday party) and filled with treats and gifts. A player is blindfolded and given a stick to use to break the piñata open and let all the treats fall out. The game is thought to have come from a religious custom in which the piñata represented evil, the stick stood for virtue, and the player represented faith. The treats were the reward for overcoming evil.

away to work on another project. Antonio would stay right where she left him, working hard on whatever job she had given him. When she returned, Antonio proudly displayed his results, such as a bucket full of weeds (and flowers) he had pulled. Sometimes he washed people's pets, sometimes he swept the floor, sometimes he watered a garden— always with a smile on his face. Accomplishing these jobs and being near his mother made Antonio happy.

Christina learned early on not to fight over every detail with Antonio. He did not understand some things, and trying to explain them to him only ended up with them both being frustrated. So sometimes he would go to work without his shoes or shirt on. Sometimes they would take the long way around to get to a place, because he insisted on it. Or sometimes he would curl up without warning and take a nap. Christina did not mind. The two of them understood each other, even if not many others did.

Most of the neighborhood respected Christina—they knew how hard she worked and saw how she struggled to take care of her son—but they stayed away from her. They didn't understand Antonio's condition and whispered about his being "bewitched."

Christina had given up on explaining it, given up on falling in love again, and given up on having more children. She had some friendly acquaintances, but not any real friends. There wasn't time to dwell on her loneliness—Antonio's care was simply full-time.

Lord, I pray for another great day ahead at *Casa de Mi Padre*. Joshua's prayer was interrupted by the ringing phone in the orphanage office. He smiled as he went to answer it, finishing his prayer quickly in his head: *Who knows if this is a call with a donation or a referral of a new child—but you, Father, are in control of this house. Lead me.*

"Bueno," Joshua said into the receiver. For Joshua, it was not just another phone call, another day at work. He glanced up at the pictures of children's artwork hung up around his desk. For him it was another chance to love the kids no one understood, the kids society would throw away or couldn't care for. It was another day to tell a child he is loved, another day of looking for moments when the light would come on in a child's eyes. It was eternal work. The work was hard; there were often more needs than he could keep up with. It was way more than full-time. But it's right where God had asked him to be. "Bueno, Casa de Mi Padre, *como puedo ayudarte hoy?*"

"Aaahhh!" Antonio heard his mother groan from another room, but didn't understand why. She was in bed. Again. He touched his stomach. He was hungry another day and didn't know what to do about it, or how to help his mother. She always gave him his jobs.

How can I get another mango like yesterday? Antonio wondered.

He looked around on the front porch where he had been spending most of his days since his mother got sick. He picked up a stick he had found in the yard. *Swish!* He swung at a bag stuffed with paper hanging from the bar above his head. He liked to pretend the bag was a piñata.

He hit at it again and again, staying there and

Como puedo ayudarte hoy? means "How can I help you today?"

playing for hours. And for a while he forgot his hunger as he focused on the bag, imagining it was a birthday piñata, stuffed with candy, all for him. Trying to break it open was like waiting for a hundred gifts to fall out.

On the other end of the phone was a government social worker, calling about a complaint received from a "concerned neighbor." This neighbor claimed a dying woman on her street had confided in her, saying she was worried that, after her death, there would be no one to care for her eight-year-old son who was "mentally disabled" and suffered from untreated epilepsy. The boy had been running around unsupervised while she had been bedridden these last months and no one had stepped in to help. The mother had told this neighbor she was planning on taking her son with her to Heaven this week, so he wouldn't be left alone. She couldn't bear to imagine him fending for himself and it seemed to her the kindest thing she could do. This neighbor knew that it wasn't right, but didn't know what else to say or do for the dying woman.

She had called to report it and wanted *someone* to do something.

Antonio saw peering faces through the sheet that hung as a door in their small shack. Maybe the faces were looking at him? talking about him? He didn't understand. They just looked in and saw him, and then, seeming satisfied, hurried away. *What do they want?* he wondered. He turned back to

*Defend the weak and the fatherless;
uphold the cause of the poor and the oppressed.*

—Psalm 82:3

the rock collection he was playing with. Then he heard his mother crying in the other room. He took her some water and carried in his rock collection to play where he could still see her. Eventually she fell asleep, and he lay down next to her with his rocks underneath him, thinking that, if those peering faces came closer, they couldn't take his rocks without him knowing it.

Joshua hung up the phone, but not without promising to investigate that very afternoon. He put his head in his hands and prayed for the boy, the mother, the neighbor, the authorities involved. He prayed for their home and his team and what they might do. He asked Jesus, *what would you have us to do? What comfort can we give this woman? Lead me. I will defend your children as you lead.* He repeated the content of the call to some of the staff. They shuddered as he shared the social worker's last words, "The mother is afraid for Antonio's future without her. She knows she is dying and she knows no one will take care of him. She is planning on killing her son, to spare him what might lie ahead." They decided to take immediate action.

Antonio woke up, still lying on those rocks, and heard his stomach growling. He looked down and realized he was undressed again, but it didn't bother him. He didn't like the way the clothes felt on his body, and he forgot where he

put them anyway. He looked around for some food and

found a tortilla; he rolled it up and ate it cold. It made him feel better for the moment.

He stood and watched his mother on the bed. Her chest lifted up and down with each breath; she was asleep. But Antonio thought her face looked funny—twisted up, like when she was angry about something, or maybe sad? He didn't know she was in pain, even in sleep.

Many homes where Antonio lived look like this.

When Joshua arrived at the home, he banged a rock against the makeshift metal gate—a common way in that region of announcing there was a visitor. He could see the house was made with scrap material found at a construction site or a garbage dump. It had four walls, a tin roof, and a big front porch area. It was nicely hidden in the shade of a tree. *It must be cooler inside,* he thought. When no one answered, he ventured inside the gate.

At first he saw the woman's eyes widen in fear when she saw the strangers enter her home. Too weak to get up, she called out in her loudest voice, "What are you doing here?"

When she learned they were from a local children's home and wanted to talk about Antonio, her eyes softened.

Joshua told her they had heard she was very sick and that she was worried about who would take care of her son after she was gone. She nodded in assent.

Antonio had retreated to a corner when the strangers came in. But he came a little closer as he heard his mother's voice. She sounded like she was telling a story, but he couldn't hear or understand all that she said.

She was telling
a story—their story.
She told them through
tears about the cancer
that was eating away at
her body, now in its late
stages. She told them

about her son's birth and the developmental delays
and severe epilepsy that made him difficult to care for
at times. She told them about his frequent seizures
and how they had learned together to cope with
them. She continued on to share how Antonio's father
had died several years ago. Antonio's aging grandmother was his only other relative now, but she too
was in no condition to care for or protect Antonio.

Tears slowly filled her eyes and slid down her
cheeks. In starts and stops, she quietly confessed what
she had planned for that very week, knowing her
days left were few. "I don't know what to do. My little
family is all alone. Who will defend us? I'm having

Epilepsy is a brain disorder that affects the nervous system and results in seizures at some point in life. Recent studies show that up to 70 percent of children and adults with newly diagnosed epilepsy are able to control the condition with medications.

trouble even thinking right now." She whispered, "Everything just hurts. You can't imagine how desperate I feel. I love Antonio, but I don't think anyone else out there will."

Joshua paused in thought, then leaned in, so the woman wouldn't miss a word. "God loves Antonio. He always has and he always will. God put that love in my heart for him, even before I met him. That's why I am here, to offer you a choice. Let me have the opportunity to love Antonio on behalf of the God who sent me here. Give me this gift."

At another time, in another place, these words might have led Joshua to launch into a Bible story he had told the children at the home some time ago. It was about Mephibosheth, the son of King David's friend Jonathan. He had been hurt as a baby and, because he could not walk, he was not valued by the people of that time. He could not work, or be a soldier, or serve the king. At this point, one of the children had asked, "So what could he do? What good was he?"

Joshua had told the children how David wanted to keep a special promise he had made to his friend before he died. It was important to the king to keep his word. So when he found out that this son of his friend still lived, he had him brought to his court, and gave him all the land that had belonged to Jonathan's family. And more than that, he would always eat at the table of the king. *Mephibosheth allowed David to fulfill his promise. He gave the king himself, and that was exactly what the king needed.* Joshua could not share all that was in his head, but he tried to put all his feeling into his brief words to the weary woman: "Please, give me this gift."

Up until that moment, in her mind, Christina had seen only two choices. One meant abandoning Antonio with no hope of anyone to take him in. It meant leaving the child she dearly loved all alone, unable to meet even his most basic needs, just hoping that by chance he would somehow learn to survive. It was unthinkable.

The other choice was to take his life before she

died. Also unthinkable. But short of a miracle, it was the choice she had settled on. Softly and slowly the sobs rose up in her until she almost choked on them. The opportunity God was offering her was unbelievable. *Has he really heard my cries, here all alone in this shack? Has he seen my pain? Does he know my fear?*

"Yes," she whispered to herself. "Yes, *Dios me escucho*." She looked over at Antonio, and could see the curve of his back hunched over his rocks—a backbone sticking out that she had traced with her fingers a thousand times. She turned back toward the man. "But can you promise me you will take care of him . . . that you will love him always?"

We love because he first loved us.

—1 John 4:19

The man held out a hand to her, and she took it. "Love him?" he said. "God is his Defender-Kinsman. Antonio is the son of the King I serve. To take care of him is like caring for the son of the One who died for me. It would be my privilege to serve him, to love him."

His words were like a healing medicine to her pain. She sighed and rested, but held tight onto his hand and onto the promise of rescue for her son.

POST CARD

CORRESPONDENCE

Dios me escucho means "God listens to me."

Joshua had been watching Antonio out of the corner of his eye this whole time. When his mother had started to cry, the boy had come forward, as if to make sure they were not hurting her. He stepped in and out of the room during the next hour, unsettled.

When the mother had settled back into a light sleep, Joshua took a closer look at the boy. At first he had been surprised to see Antonio had no clothes on, but he understood the battle of dressing a child who resisted. He knew the mother didn't have that strength anymore. *Besides getting him dressed, what other battles might lie ahead?* Joshua wondered. He watched in silence as Antonio swung a stick at a cardboard box that had been hung on a frayed string from a beam above. Joshua considered how Antonio had been able to get the box up there to attach it. *Did someone help him? What was he doing?*

Once comfortable with the presence of the strangers, Antonio stepped out onto the porch, found his favorite stick, and began to wildly swing it through the air at his "piñata." The bag from earlier was now destroyed, lying in pieces on the ground, but the box would take longer to knock down. Antonio liked to pretend it was just like the ones he played with as a small boy. He closed his eyes and saw all the bright colors of those special presents and dreamed up the candy and treats that would be inside. He hit at the box again and again, wishing hard that this time something good would fall out.

The man who had been talking to his mother now spoke to him. He pointed to the hanging box and asked, "Where did it come from?"

Antonio was a bit startled by the question. He thought maybe he was in trouble. He pointed behind the house, at the neighbor's trash heap. Then he went back to striking at the box. He hoped they would not take away his treasure.

Bam! Bam! Over and over the boy hit the box, but Joshua could see he was not angry, just determined. He remembered something the woman had told them about Antonio's father bringing gifts for the boy and realized then what Antonio was doing. *Lord, what gift do you have to offer him today? I know it must be better than anything he could get from his pretend piñata.* Joshua stepped back into the shack and sat for a while longer in the room with Antonio's mother, soaking in the environment, wanting her to feel comfortable.

She lay quietly on her soiled sheet, slipping in and out of sleep, a shadow of a woman. The room was dark, with no electric lights, and a window shade drawn. While she rested, he looked full on her face. He could hardly make it out, it was so dark, but he could see her expression had relaxed in the last hour. She was suffering physically from her illness, but it was easy to see her greatest suffering was the burden she had carried in her heart for her son's future.

Her tiny frame struggled for breath as she opened her eyes off and on to focus on Joshua and his team who had come to help. He sat close so he could hear her whispers and so she could see his face as he and the others explained what life in their home was like.

They told her about *Casa de Mi Padre*, a home where children were welcome, wanted, worthy, and loved, regardless of their abilities or disabilities. They offered her the promise of hope for Antonio as part of a family who would care for him, love him, and who would actually want him.

Christina listened intently, thinking over and over, *There is an alternative. There is another way.*

"Our home is full of children just like Antonio. We have green grass where the children run and play. We love the children and care for them, especially the special parts of them. We want them to live a life full of hope, regardless of their special needs."

The words sounded so good to her, she could hardly believe them. "Is there even such a place?" she asked, her voice cracking and shaking. "Have you seen Antonio, do you understand how special he is?"

"I can see him right now," the man named Joshua answered, as he took his gaze off her to

POST CARD

CORRESPONDENCE

Casa de Mi Padre means "My Father's House."

watch for a moment the curious boy who had moved back into the room. "But more importantly, God sees him and called us to come here this afternoon to tell you there is another way. . . . Would you like a few days to think about it?"

"I don't need to think about it anymore." Christina's fragile face slowly melted into a soft smile of relief as she turned toward Joshua. "If your Defender-Kinsman will take care of him, he can go."

Before she returned to a merciful sleep, she whispered a tearful good-bye to her son, who didn't understand much of what was happening that day. She didn't want him to see her die, and she knew the timing was God-planned, but it increased her pain all the more to see him go. As her guests stood back and looked on from a respectful distance, she could feel the weight of his care slide from her shoulders to theirs.

Joshua prayed into the air, thick with emotion, "Defender God, be with this sister, bring her your comfort, on every level. Take her home to be with you in your perfect timing. And thank you for showing us how much you value Antonio and for bringing him into our story today."

Joshua gathered up a few things for Antonio to bring to the ranch, items not of monetary value but of emotional value, and listened as his grandmother tried to explain to the boy what would happen next. She listed off things she knew would interest her grandson—all the benefits of living in the children's home. Joshua knew the gifts Antonio would receive were more intangible than food and grass and shelter. In the weeks and months ahead, he would receive education, security, and medical care. But whatever would help Antonio with this first step was more important.

Antonio stared down at his rock collection as his grandmother spoke. "You will have food to eat, grass to play in, a school to go to, your own bed . . ."

My own bed? What kind of bed? What kind of food? What kind of school? Antonio had lots of questions in his mind, but he did not say anything. He had been to preschool once for a few times years ago, and he had only a vague idea of what school was like. Sometimes he and his mother had walked by a school when they were going to a job together. He remembered seeing groups of children playing games, shouting and laughing.

But for months now Antonio had hardly left his

house. Why was his grandmother talking about him leaving? By himself? He did not understand it. He knew his mother was very sick. Grandmother said his mother would soon be *con Dios*. Antonio wondered, *Where is that? And why can't I go with her?*

As his grandmother spoke in gentle tones, he moved closer to his mother's side. He lined his rocks up quietly on the mat beside her body. Then he laid his head down on her chest and put his arms around her neck.

"*Te amo, mi hijo*," his mother finally whispered. Antonio wrapped his arms tighter around her. *Please don't leave me!* The words were in his head, but he said nothing as the strangers pulled his arms away.

POST CARD

CORRESPONDENCE

If someone close to you has died, you know it is sometimes hard to understand, and hard to talk about. What would you have told Antonio to help him understand?

Con Dios means "with God."

In spite of all that Antonio had missed out on in his eight years of life, it was clear that he had certainly *not* missed out on the love of a family who had done their best to care for him. As they said their good-byes, Joshua could see plainly how dearly Antonio's mother and grandmother loved the boy, and how much Antonio loved them in return.

But it was time to go now. Joshua could see the dying woman's face growing more weary. He and another staff member took hold of Antonio's arms as gently as they could and pried him away from his mother's neck.

Antonio resisted being led away, dragging his bare feet over the splintery wood, and he pushed and pulled as they tried to put him into the car. *Had he ever been in a car?* Joshua wondered. He sat in the back seat with the boy and comforted him as best he could while Antonio flailed about. Finally, as the car pulled away, the frightened boy began to cry, with deep, choking sobs.

Lord, lead us. Joshua prayed the whole way home. *Help him to see you. Help him to imagine what you have waiting for him, something far better than what he can pretend. Comfort him. Hold him. Thank you for being the giver of all good gifts, and for your provision and protection for Antonio today.*

When they arrived at the home, Antonio was worn out. The man in the car and a nice woman showed him to a room and pointed to a bed with a soft pillow and blankets. They told him that was where he would sleep and that he would share the room with a few other boys. But he was so tired and scared, he just curled up on the floor and fell fast asleep there. He was used to sleeping on the floor.

The next few days seemed to go by in a blur. Antonio learned about the building where he would live and learn and eat and play, and he explored the area around the home, where the other kids played sports on the grass outside. He met all the other children and tried to remember some of their names.

POST CARD

CORRESPONDENCE

Te amo, mi hijo means "I love you, my son."

This is a room in the home where Antonio lives today.

One of the workers seemed to be always with him wherever he went in those first several days. As he spent time with them, Antonio grew to be friendlier and talked more. They were very kind to him and gave him things to do that he liked very much. They were always asking if he needed anything.

Before long, Antonio had found ways he could be helpful by picking up toys, helping to sort laundry items, or sweeping or mopping the floor. He felt so good to be doing jobs again. It reminded him of the times he had spent with his mother, and how proud she had been of him. He wanted her to be proud.

Later that week, after Antonio had come to live at Casa de Mi Padre, Joshua received another call. It was the same social worker whose call had brought Antonio into their lives. "She's gone. Antonio's mother passed in the night. The grandmother contacted me yesterday. Without either parent and an elderly grandmother . . . I am afraid he will never have any other living arrangement available to him. Are you doing OK? Is he doing OK?"

"Am I doing OK?" Joshua repeated. "Yes! God has been faithful to us all. It feels like Antonio is home. It's not been easy, but it's been good. We are trying our best to love him in a way that honors his mother and the God who defends him." Joshua looked out the window and smiled at the children playing in the yard. "You should see him play in the grass we told his mother about. There are plenty of rocks for his collection, a few real piñatas we have found, and lots of children he is learning to interact with."

His voice caught for a moment, then he continued, "His life was spared for a reason, of that I am sure. He has great purpose and great value. To have him at our table, to have a front-row seat to his story—for that, I thank you. Thank you for bringing us into it."

The social worker hung up the phone that day, shaking her head at Joshua's response and at a love she didn't understand. Yet.

But Antonio's life had already done so much to show others about God's love. God ministered in one week through Antonio to his mother, showing her in her last days that there is a God who hears. He ministered to the grandmother, to Antonio himself, and to the neighbor who wondered if she had done the right thing. He ministered to Joshua and his staff, who watched God move, to the other children, and to all those who met Antonio.

And now God is ministering to us, who can read his story. God saved Antonio because he loves him, and that love is a huge light, pointing others to a God who cares, who provides, who protects, who defends.

Today, Antonio is fifteen years old. He now keeps his clothes on, although he still needs help buttoning, and he receives frequent reminders about his shoes being on the wrong feet. He goes to a special school, which he loves, and where he is loved by his teachers and friends. He has a wonderful sense of humor and loves to tease and give hugs. He also enjoys his chores, especially mopping the floor!

Now, filled up with the love of his Father, Antonio is a giver of gifts, a vessel for that love to others. Antonio welcomes all the new children into the home with hugs and smiles.

REMEMBER THIS

When you ask, "What can I give?" just remember that you can't outspend God. His economy is different from ours; when you pour out, he more than fills you back up. When you give yourself to others, he makes you feel even fuller than when you started. He'll bring people and relationships into your life you might not have ever imagined (or chosen!), but if God brings them into your path, it's because he wants to bless you in ways you would have otherwise missed out on!

As one of the oldest children, he is a helper to the workers and has a spirit of service that is contagious to the other children. Antonio understands he has a special place in his home and in this big family. He is being taught and teaching others that in Jesus we are all welcomed, wanted, loved, and worthy to be defended. And he is glad to have a seat at this table, every day.

James 1:17 says: "Every good and perfect gift is from above, coming down from the Father of the heavenly lights, who does not change like shifting shadows."

What is the best gift you've ever received? What gifts have you received from God? Have you ever had something happen to you that you didn't know was a gift until later on?

Write your thoughts about Antonio's story here. Think about what you have to give.

Chapter 3

CAITLYN'S TRUTH

As her teacher paced slowly around the classroom, Caitlyn's heart raced. She sank a little lower in her seat, resting her cheek on her hand. *Have I got it all covered? Will she see?* She kept her head down and focused on the paper in front of her. But no matter how many times she read the questions, she couldn't think of the answers. *What is wrong with my brain?*

She was starting to believe the kids who teased her on the bus every day. Maybe she *was* an idiot. They had been merciless again this morning, especially when the leader had caught sight of the purple mark on the side of her face. "What happened to your face? Is that your idea of a makeover? Or did you just run into your door again?" Caitlyn never understood why they thought they were so funny. But their laughter hurt her, like hammers banging on the inside of her brain. She just tried to ignore them, counting

the houses passing by on the dreary city street, hoping they would get bored of watching her and just leave her alone.

It had taken her several extra minutes to find where they had thrown her backpack this time, which made her late getting off the bus, so she ran to get to the doors on time. She didn't want another tardy. *If I get one more, they'll call my mom*, she thought. She knew her mom would be angry—she hated coming in for conferences. She hated it so much, she'd told Caitlyn that next time she'd just go and tell them everything, and Caitlyn would be taken away.

"Is that what you want?" Her mother's words played over and over again in her head.

It was *not* what Caitlyn wanted. But nothing was the way she wanted it to be. She just wanted a normal family. A mom, a dad, a grandma. If she just kept saying the right things, maybe her dream of a family would come true.

"Caitlyn, can I see you outside a moment?" Her teacher's voice at her side startled her, and she forgot to keep her cheek covered up. *Oh, no.* Caitlyn steeled herself as she walked out of the classroom, silently running through the rehearsed answers she knew so well.

"Maybe, Sheryl, we will have to add another brother or sister to this house. We should adopt!" That was the first time she remembered hearing about adoption, from her new stepdad. But they were just words. No such thing ever happened in her family—it was another empty promise, like the station wagon, and the pink room, and the puppy she was supposed to get. In fact, her parents' new marriages marked the beginning of a long, difficult season for her.

But in that season, a seed was planted. She'd always loved babies. And helping kids who had it worse than her was something that had rolled around in her mind for a long while. But at age ten, there wasn't much she could do about it.

Despite the problems her parents and stepparents were having, Sheryl's world felt complete with her big brothers in it. When they came to know Jesus and shared him with her, it was wonderful—mainly because *they* were wonderful. Years later, when Sheryl got into a difficult situation and became pregnant, it was her brothers who assured her that each life had value—a lesson she's still grateful for. They held their sister and her baby girl at the birth. It was a scene Sheryl would remember vividly later in life.

Eventually, Sheryl married a man who would adopt her daughter, and the three became a family. But her long-time stirring to care for children who needed families did not go away. She talked about these feelings with her husband, and he listened and sympathized, but gently reminded her that he already was caring for a child not his own. He rejoiced with her when they had two sons together.

But inside of Sheryl, a voice kept saying, *My heart is growing! I want to, I need to help unwanted babies and struggling moms!*

Caitlyn's mom, Heather, was fidgety. *How long has it been since I used? An hour? All morning?* She didn't know, didn't remember. Whenever she hadn't used drugs for a while, hours ran together. She just kept looking for the next time she could satisfy her craving, her addiction. *Was it time to get Caitlyn from school? Was today a school day?* She looked across the street and wondered if the lady who lived there was home. She usually was there when Caitlyn got off the bus, and took care of the girl until Heather returned from wherever she had gone.

Caitlyn probably just goes there first now

anyway, Heather thought. *I sure haven't been there for her lately.* A little flash of guilt surfaced, but Heather pushed it back down, stamping out another cigarette in the plate full of ash. *She'll be OK. After all, my mom left me and I was OK. You've got to learn to look out for yourself at some point—no one's going to do it for you.*

She thought about the bruise on Caitlyn's cheek that was still there this morning. Heather's jaw tightened as scenes from the night before ran through her brain. *He didn't mean to hurt her.* That's what she told herself, anyway. Caitlyn was always asking so many questions. Anthony just got tired of her talking. He wasn't used to being around kids like Caitlyn. *If*

POST CARD

CORRESPONDENCE

Child abuse is defined as any act which results in serious physical or emotional harm to a child. If you suspect abuse, talk to your parent or guardian or a teacher about it. In the U.S., you can call 1-800-4-A-CHILD (1-800-422-4453) to report child abuse or neglect.

she would just be quiet! But she'll keep her mouth shut today, I know she will. She always protects us. She's just got to keep her stories straight . . . Her mind wandered as she automatically lit another cigarette. She felt a wave of nausea and clutched at her stomach with her free hand. *I need something stronger than this.*

About a third of the children in foster care are between the ages of six and twelve. The average number of birthdays a child spends in foster care is two. (From www .kidsarewaiting.org.)

POST CARD

CORRESPONDENCE

Addiction is a physical and mental impairment in which a person develops a compulsive need for and the habitual use of a habit-forming substance. An addicted person has great difficulty stopping "using" on his or her own, and often needs the help of doctors, counselors, family, and friends.

I'm starving! After serving all morning at church in the nursery, Sheryl was ready for lunch. She couldn't wait to tell her husband about the little blond-haired boy and his foster mom she had met that day. He was born so sick—"Addicted to drugs," the mom had said—but was now getting stronger each week. His foster mom said the little boy didn't have much hope when they picked him up from the hospital; he needed a lot of help with his withdrawal symptoms. She warned Sheryl that he might cry a lot in the nursery. Sheryl wasn't sure what kind of withdrawal symptoms a baby could experience, but she had plenty of hope and help! She held the baby the whole time he was in the nursery, and he didn't cry—not even once.

She started in on the story excitedly with her husband as they got the kids settled in the restaurant booth. But her enthusiasm plummeted when she saw the look in his eyes. She hadn't even mentioned the idea of fostering again yet, but her husband knew her heart.

"Not now. Not yet . . . maybe not ever. I'm happy for them, and really happy for the boy, but we have our hands full here." As he spoke, he rescued one of their sons from being poked with a fork by the other and handed their daughter her cell phone. "If it's God's will, he'll change my heart. You can be praying for that."

No problem, thought Sheryl, and smiled. She already was.

Even though her mom wore baggy clothes, Caitlyn couldn't help noticing that her belly was getting bigger every week. One night when she was struggling over homework, she looked over at her mom munching on chips. She took a deep breath and blurted out her question: "Mom, are you pregnant?"

Heather barely glanced at Caitlyn. She stuffed another handful of chips in her mouth before making her muffled reply. "Yes." She kept chewing and snapped, "Finish your homework."

Caitlyn turned back to the worksheet and started writing down random answers. It didn't matter—her mom wouldn't check it anyway, and her teachers didn't seem to care much what she did anymore.

POST CARD

CORRESPONDENCE

Foster care is parental care provided to a child who is not tied to the foster parent by blood or legal ties. The word foster comes from the Old English fostor, meaning "food, nourishment." Foster parents often need to give their children physical, mental, emotional, and spiritual nourishment.

Besides, she couldn't stop thinking about the baby.

Anthony, her mom's last "boyfriend," had been gone for several weeks. There wasn't much food in the house—Caitlyn had gone without dinner more than a few times. She knew her mom would need lots of food for the baby growing inside her, and she wondered how she could help.

Despite her hunger, and the stress in the house, and strangers coming in and out at all hours, and all the lies she had had to tell to keep them "safe," Caitlyn's heart swelled with new hope. *Maybe this new baby will be a good thing. Maybe Mom will stop the drugs now. Maybe we can be a real family.* She loved the idea of having a little brother or sister to play with, to teach stuff to, and to protect. Caitlyn sneaked another look at her mom's belly and wondered how long it would be before the baby would be here. She could hardly wait.

Sheryl worked in the nursery almost every Sunday. And every week, she had a new story to report about how the blond baby boy and his foster mom were doing. He was eating better, he had rolled over, he had stopped crying so much at night. . . . Even though she was just giving the weekly update, she could feel the question behind her words each time, and she knew her husband could feel it too: *Can we try this sometime—please?*

One week, they were sitting in that same restaurant booth when her husband looked around at their three healthy, happy, and maybe a little bit loud, kids, and cleared his throat. Sheryl gazed back at him as he said to her, "This is not yes, or even now. But . . ." As he paused, Sheryl twisted her napkin under the table and tried to calm her racing heart. "Let's take the first step and get informed."

Months went by, and nothing really changed. Caitlyn knew her mom was still doing drugs, even though she made half-hearted attempts to hide it from her. There were still strange faces. And there were still so many lies.

They had moved in with Heather's grandmother, who lived close by. "Nana" seemed old to Caitlyn, and a little strange, but Caitlyn liked her. She was good at doing the "mom stuff" that her mom never seemed to be able to do. But she had no control over Heather.

Caitlyn felt angry with her mom a lot of the time. She had lots of questions: *Why can't she be nicer to Nana? Why did she invite those people over— couldn't she see Nana needed to rest? Why can't she be like other moms?* She was only ten years old, but many times, she felt like she was more grown-up than her own mother.

As the due date came closer, Heather seemed to get even worse. She would stay in bed for whole days and didn't even notice when Caitlyn came in to check on her. Her brain was so confused with drugs, she couldn't think straight. Sometimes she couldn't even put a few words together. But often when she did, she would remind Caitlyn, "Keep our secrets."

Information led to classes, and classes led to certification, and soon, to her delight, Sheryl's family was learning firsthand about fostering.

Their first little guy was two years old. They knew he would be with them only a short time while his father waited for a judge's orders to go through. This dad had not known his son until several months ago, when children's services took custody of him from his mother, who struggled with mental illness.

It was sad to let the boy go, but when the day came, Sheryl's heart swelled as she watched father and son reunite. It seemed so natural when the toddler jumped out of her lap and ran to his daddy. There was not a dry eye in the house; it was beautiful.

It also made Sheryl think harder about how she could help her foster children's families. They weren't horrible people—they were people in difficult stories, just like she had once been. Maybe they didn't have the support she did, but maybe in the same way her brothers had reached out to her, she could reach out to these families.

They had other children come after that, and Sheryl's heart was broken more than once. But each time, she felt she was part of a bigger story. On the day of one particularly difficult good-bye, Sheryl prayed, *Lord, this is hard. Good, but hard. Should we take a break? Can we keep doing this? Is this what you are asking of us?* She stared out the window where she had watched the family drive away with the delightful little girl she had loved caring for. *Is there someone else you have waiting for us?*

Within a week, she had an answer.

Through the fog of her mind, Caitlyn's mom felt the pain of labor. Somehow, she managed to get to a hospital and stumbled inside. She gave birth to a baby boy. His first cries were the hungry cries of an addict.

Heather said little after coming back from the hospital. She just sat on the couch, staring into space, smoking one cigarette after another. Finally, Caitlyn couldn't stand not knowing any longer. She wondered why no baby had come home. "Did the baby . . . survive?"

Her mom only nodded yes and looked away.

Later, Caitlyn's great-grandma explained. "You know the people who used to come around and ask questions? The ones who've asked you things at school before?"

Caitlyn nodded.

"Those people are at hospitals too. When babies are born sick, they know the mothers are sick too—

From Beth's Journal

When I met Sheryl, I couldn't believe her courage. There are easier story lines she could have chosen, lines that would have made her life simpler—but she didn't want simple. She and her husband wanted frontline action in a battle for the hearts of today's fatherless. Those are the best stories, when you are in over your head and you cry out to God! He will always come through. He will always get his way. He is always defending.

Do you want to help struggling families? With a parent's permission, check out Safe Families for Children (www.safe-families.org) and see how you, your family, and your church can work together to help families in crisis situations.

too sick to take care of a newborn baby. So they take the babies for a while, to take care of them."

Caitlyn felt afraid again. Afraid those people would come talk to her. Afraid of more questions. Afraid of more lying. And afraid for her little baby brother. She wondered if she would ever get to see him now. *Where is he?*

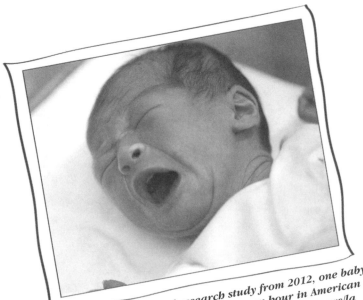

According to a medical research study from 2012, one baby is born addicted to drugs about once an hour in American hospitals. (http://articles.latimes.com/2012/apr/30/news/la-heb-neonatal-abstinence-syndrome-20120430)

When Sheryl got the call about a little heroin-addicted baby boy, she said yes immediately. It was as if all the questions she had been having about fostering melted away.

Poor little Anthony Jr., as he was called, had spent six weeks in the hospital as the doctors and nurses took care of him. And because of his need for the drug that had been in his mother's body, he had cried. A lot. The nurses had tried to comfort him when they could, but there were other babies who needed care. And Anthony had had very few visitors.

No one to hold him. No one to love him. Sometimes he would scream for hours. Twelve hours. Every day.

When the baby boy came to Sheryl's home, she knew his troubles. She knew he needed to be weaned off the drugs in his body. And she knew the drugs might have already damaged his brain.

Sheryl and her whole family took in the little boy as one of their own from the moment he arrived. She wore him in a baby sling around her body all day long when he was awake. She prayed for him, sang him to sleep, managed his medications, and kept records of his food intake and dirty diapers. He was held, kissed, hugged, played with, and loved on every day.

He hardly ever cried.

Sheryl knew little about the boy's birth family, but after a while she found out that Anthony (or Cameron, as they had come to call him) had an older sister. It took many attempts, but she finally was able to reach the girl's guardian and arrange a time for Caitlyn to come meet her baby brother.

When Nana told her she was going to see her baby brother, Caitlyn was happy, but scared again. She wondered what this family would be like. Would they ask her questions too?

But by the second visit, Caitlyn had already started looking forward to seeing her brother and the woman who was taking care of him, Sheryl. Sheryl listened to her stories and never got irritated with her when she asked questions.

You will know the truth, and the truth will set you free.
—John 8:32

The next time they met, Caitlyn brought pictures she had drawn for her brother, and she was surprised to see two other boys there, about her age. Sheryl introduced her sons. Caitlyn felt shy at first, but soon she found herself talking and laughing with the boys. They asked her lots of questions, but they were good questions, like what she liked to do and how far she could kick a soccer ball. They were questions she could answer on her own, without having to remember certain words to say.

But when school started, the visits stopped. Caitlyn was sad about this. It had been so nice to spend time with a real family, and she missed seeing her baby brother. Caitlyn felt angry too. She didn't want to go back to school—back to being bullied, and fighting over homework she couldn't do, and pretending to be OK, when she wasn't at all.

Her mother had never come on any of the visits. Caitlyn didn't really understand why. She heard her mother talking on the phone once, saying something about how "they'd throw me in jail the first chance they got." She was afraid to ask about it. Her mom was nervous and cranky a lot these days, and often gone.

But then a call came. Nana told her Sheryl had asked if Caitlyn would like to go with the family to a fall festival the next weekend. Caitlyn had never been to a festival! She was full of questions, but Nana seemed hesitant. "Please, Nana, please!! Can I go? Please?" As she often did when Caitlyn whined like this, Nana gave in.

It was a bad week. Caitlyn's backpack was stolen, and she failed two quizzes. At home, there was little to eat. Nana had gone shopping last Sunday, but Caitlyn's mom had come home that night with "friends," and the next day a lot of the food was gone—even Caitlyn's favorite cereal that her great-grandma had let her buy.

Worst of all, her mom had threatened to not let her go on the trip. She said mean things about Sheryl and her family. She said they were trying to take Caitlyn away.

Caitlyn wondered if that would be so bad.

By the time Saturday came, Caitlyn was a

mixed-up bundle of excitement and nerves and stress and smiles. Her mom had left just before

Sheryl and her family arrived. When Sheryl got out of their car, she handed the baby to great-grandma so she could have some time with him, and they all walked inside. It was the first time they had been in Caitlyn's home.

Sheryl and her husband, Larry, looked at all the pictures on the walls and made comments about what a beautiful family they had. Sheryl stopped for several moments in front of a picture of Caitlyn's mom holding Caitlyn as a baby. "Your mom is so pretty," she said to Caitlyn. Caitlyn thought of the way her mom had looked this morning and wondered if Sheryl would

say that if she could see her right now.

When they had finished looking through several photo albums that Nana had pulled out, they got ready to go. Sheryl gave Nana a quick hug as she took the baby back. Caitlyn thought her great-grandma looked happier than she had looked all week, maybe all year. As they pulled away in the van, Caitlyn waved good-bye to Nana through the window. Though she was still excited about going on the trip, she felt something like a dark cloud on her mind. It was a feeling she always got when she felt like she was going to mess something up, or right before she and her mom got into a fight, or when she knew she was going to have to lie.

On the way to the festival, Sheryl prayed hard that God would guide her in what to do. She had warned her kids not to ask Caitlyn too much about her family, but after seeing all those photos this morning, and smelling the pungent smell of cigarette smoke in the air (a sure sign that the girl's mother had been there recently), she found it difficult herself to hold her tongue and not try to pry more information out of the girl.

When they got to the place, Sheryl realized immediately why the caseworkers had warned them about Caitlyn's behavior problems. Caitlyn wandered off wherever she wanted to go, pretending not to hear them when they called. She knocked things over "on accident," and threw handfuls of hay into the air (getting it all over the other kids). She wouldn't talk to the two boys, who were so close to her own age, and relentlessly pestered Sheryl's older daughter instead.

After going to dinner, made late by Caitlyn's antics, Sheryl and Larry dropped Caitlyn off.

Sheryl sighed on the way home, and Larry asked if she was as exhausted as he was. "I am tired," she answered, "but mostly sad. Sad for Caitlyn. Sad for Nana. Sad for that whole family. And sad that we can't do more to help. I thought having Caitlyn spend time with our family would be good, but now . . ." Her voice trailed off as she glanced in the visor mirror at her sons, who had nodded off already, and her daughter, who sat quietly staring out the window. "I just don't know."

Caitlyn knew she had not behaved her best on the family outing. She had tried, but she felt so angry inside sometimes, she just didn't care what happened. As the days passed by and no more calls came from Sheryl, Caitlyn became depressed. *So that was it. No trips now.*

Then a few days later, Sheryl did call. She wanted to know if Caitlyn could go out with them again. Nana agreed, grateful for something to occupy Caitlyn and distract her from the downward spiral her mother was on.

But when Heather found out about the plans, she refused to let Caitlyn go. "I'm going to a wedding on Saturday and Caitlyn's going with me. I want her there."

That was that. Nana argued with her, but she stubbornly stormed off. Without a word to Caitlyn, Nana came inside and called Sheryl to tell her Caitlyn wouldn't be able to go with their family that weekend.

Caitlyn was confused. She wanted to see Sheryl's

family, but these days she was glad to hear that her mother wanted her . . . anywhere.

When Saturday afternoon came, Caitlyn's mom shouted at her to hurry up, stuffing tissues and gum and other junk into her purse as she walked out the door. Caitlyn picked out clothes as best as she could, said good-bye to Nana, and went outside. A wave of fear hit her as she saw her mother in the driver's seat, running her hands nervously around the steering wheel. *She doesn't even have a driver's license anymore!* Caitlyn was worried—what if a policeman stopped them? Her mom would go to jail for sure.

"Get in! We're going to miss the party!" Heather screeched.

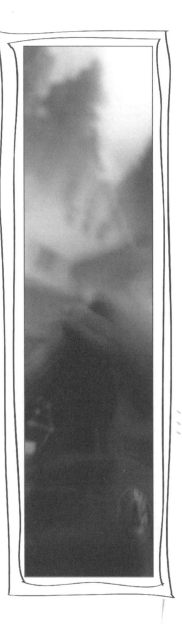

When Sheryl got off the phone after talking to Caitlyn's great-grandma, she couldn't stop worrying. The older woman had seemed upset. Sheryl had tried to ask some casual questions about the wedding Caitlyn would be attending—How far away was it? Were they going with some other family members? But the grandmother had dodged her questions and got off the phone quickly.

As the weekend approached, Sheryl's fears grew. She couldn't stop thinking about Caitlyn. She wanted to call someone, tell someone to stop Heather, sound an alarm—something! But she didn't have any real proof of any wrong being done. Should she call the caseworker and risk getting Caitlyn's mother into trouble for no reason?

She picked up the baby she now felt was completely hers and looked into his eyes. *What if something happens to your sister?*

That was it. She had to do something. She picked up the phone. *God, you've always protected my family,* Sheryl prayed. *Help me be Caitlyn's defender today.*

Monday morning came. Though the day was warm, Caitlyn wore a long-sleeved shirt and a jacket with a hood. She knew the teachers would likely make her pull her hood down, but she hoped her hair could cover the scraped up skin on the side of her face. She figured her sleeve would cover the big lumpy bandage she had stuck on her elbow.

She stared at herself in the mirror and started rehearsing in her mind. *If anyone asks what happened, just tell them . . . tell them . . .what?*

TELL THEM.

Tell? Tell the *truth*? Goose bumps prickled her skin. It was something she'd thought about doing, usually just when she was mad at her mother. But today she didn't feel angry. Just sad. Sad that her mom was an addict, and that she cared more about partying with her friends than getting her daughter home safely.

POST CARD

PON ENCE

Caseworkers are trained social workers who are assigned to deal directly with the specific issues of an individual in need of help or welfare. With foster children, caseworkers have a duty first to protect children and to find the best possible home situations for them.

REMEMBER THIS

Telling the truth is hard. Sometimes it's not about the difference between good and bad, just between good and better. But it's always the right thing to do. Whether you tell it or it forces its way out, the truth will always surface. Being a truth teller is an important part of our stories. It always leads to a better ending. When we go with truth, it always takes us on a better path.

She still couldn't believe her mom had sent her home late Saturday night with a complete stranger. A complete stranger who had shoved her out of the car on the road in front of her home and just left her there. She had been terrified, lying on the road in the dark.

What would happen to her next time? If she didn't tell someone, maybe next time she wouldn't even make it home.

She didn't want to hurt Nana, or leave her alone. She didn't want to hurt her mom either. She thought about her baby brother and Sheryl and her family. *Would they even want me? Would they believe me?*

Her mind was full of lies. Lies she had told, and lies she had been told. Answers she had to remember. Answers that had to match other lies she had already given. Her head started pounding.

But maybe it wouldn't even matter. Maybe no one

would notice her, like so many other times. Maybe no one would ask her questions.

Maybe no one cared.

Sheryl picked up the phone and her heart started racing. It was the caseworker's voice. "Hi Sheryl, I'm at Caitlyn's school, and she is ready to go! She wants to know if she can go to your house."

Tears rolled down Sheryl's cheeks as a flood of emotions rushed over her. *Thank you, God! Thank you for the truth. And thank you for defending your child.* She swallowed hard before answering, "Of course, she can! Tell her we'll be expecting her. We can't wait till she comes home."

When Caitlyn finally arrived at Sheryl's house that evening, Sheryl put Cameron on the floor so the girl could play with her baby brother while she got some dinner for Caitlyn. As she prepared things in the kitchen, the caseworker filled her in on the details of Caitlyn's weekend. She told her about her meeting with her at the school, and how brave and honest Caitlyn had been—taking the caseworker completely by surprise!

But as the night went on, after the caseworker left and Sheryl had some time alone with Caitlyn and her baby brother, more truth spilled out, one story after another.

It is estimated that between 115,000 and 130,000 children in the U.S. are waiting right now for permanent homes.

Immediately, Caitlyn understood something was very different about Sheryl's family. First off, they all ate together—every night! And they prayed together. She couldn't understand who they thought they were talking to exactly, but that was OK. They also played together. She loved being with Cameron every day and rushed home from school to see him.

The best part? Not lying and not guessing. Sheryl was always open to answering Caitlyn's questions, whether they were about her mom, or her new school, or anything at all.

Days became weeks and weeks turned into months. Caitlyn settled into a new school and a new routine. She could feel something was happening—something good. The dark cloud still came over her sometimes, and she still got into trouble every now and then, but she felt safe in this house. At home.

She had started to actually like school. Sheryl and Larry helped her with her homework, and were so proud of her when she came home with her first good grade on a test. They made sure she studied when she was supposed to, and that she got plenty of rest. They washed her clothes for her every week, and she never had to wear things that were dirty or torn or stained. She never had to go without a meal.

And she never had to go without love. She had three brothers now and a sister, and a mom and a dad.

A real family.

Sheryl and her husband could feel something different happening; it was not the same as other foster situations. A family was forming, an older sister, two brothers, a developing baby, and a shy little girl.

Each child in their family had a story, each one had a case in the hands of the Defender. Sheryl couldn't imagine this unit being broken up now. Even in the challenging times, learning to deal with a girl who had had no structure, no discipline, and not ever enough attention, Sheryl saw the power that God brought to her and her family. They were better for knowing Caitlyn and Cameron, and better for loving them. The situation had stopped feeling temporary long before the social worker called.

"Sheryl, Caitlyn's mom has gone from bad to worse. The judge will be ruling shortly on whether her parental rights are to be terminated." There was a long pause. "I just wanted to give you and Larry a chance to think about your relationship with Cameron and Caitlyn. Have you thought about adoption?"

Sheryl's heart soared. Thought about it? Only since she was ten years old. She smiled as she recalled the many times she had asked God to use her, whether for a season, or forever. Now forever was here, and it couldn't feel more right.

"Yes."

When Caitlyn found out she was going to be living with Sheryl and Larry for good, it was exactly what she wanted. A mom, a dad . . . a normal family for her and her brother. And she didn't even have to say the right things to make this dream happen. All she had to do was tell the truth.

When Sheryl asked her if she would like to be their daughter forever, Caitlyn didn't have to rehearse the answer she knew so well.

"Yes."

REMEMBER THIS

Foster children are in every school, every community. We want them in every church, and in our families—they are the fatherless and motherless right here in our country. What can we do? We can be open to fostering or adoption. We can look for struggling families in our communities and provide meals, care, and clothing. We can invite foster kids to events, parties, dinners, and playdates. We can let them know they are seen, wanted, heard, and loved.

Would you describe Caitlyn as brave? Why or why not? Do you think being truthful requires courage?

In the book of Esther, we read about a queen who wanted to protect her people, her family. First she tried to do this through secrecy, but then she stepped out in faith and truth, saying, "If I perish, I perish" (Esther 4:16).

What similarities between Caitlyn's story and Esther's do you see? Write your thoughts about Caitlyn's story here.

Chapter 4
JORANI'S JOURNEY

Mekong means "mother of waters." It's a fitting name for the river that runs all the way through Cambodia. *How many villages were born from this river? How many draw life from it?* wondered Jorani, as she finished bathing in the knee-deep water. *Someday maybe I will find out.*

From where she stood, she could see her uncles casting out their fishing nets, and close by a young boy collected water in a bucket for the small crop of rice his family grew behind their hut. The dry season had come, and everyone depended on the river for water for plants, and for the washing, drinking, and fishing that continued all year. Though they had to build their huts high up on stilts to protect them-selves from the occasional flooding, the people of these river villages, like the generations before them, chose to be near the water that sustained them.

A bittersweet memory hit the young woman as she finished bathing and gathered the rest of her clothing. It was an image of her mother, her hair falling over her face as she bent down to help a much younger Jorani bathe in these same waters. *I have no mother now but this river*, Jorani thought, as she gathered the rest of her clothes and walked up the small hill to check on her grandmother.

Before she had gone far, she found herself humming a song she had heard other villagers singing yesterday; the song had stuck in her head and was driving her crazy! But the village needed songs like this one to distract itself from its weary existence—music was one of the few ways the struggling people could entertain themselves. The reality there was harsh—always more people than food, always more memories of struggle than of refuge. Families lived together, but not well. Jorani's uncles and their families were

One of the world's longest rivers, the Mekong begins in the mountains of Tibet, flows across Myanmar and Laos PDR, and down through Thailand to Cambodia, before it reaches Vietnam and the South China Sea—a journey of some 4,350 km (about 2,700 miles). Fifty-five million people depend on the river.

in constant conflict. They tried to escape, to consider other options, but nothing they could take or do would change their stories.

Jorani knew that Buddhist teachings would say their suffering was a product of their own karma, their own ignorance. But Jorani sometimes wondered how people who had suffered so much could be expected to learn and grow on their own, when some days it was hard just to eat and sleep and breathe.

Her heavy thoughts were interrupted by the giggles of her three little sisters, who came running out of the family hut. She greeted them in the traditional manner by bowing at the waist and bringing her palms together at chest level. They responded in the same manner and began singing along with her as she continued on the path.

Jorani was pleased to see them so happy. *Today is a good day.* Some days were OK, like this one, when it seemed as though the girls had woken up and forgotten to grieve. Other days, living without their parents was brutal, and Jorani had to spend a lot of time comforting her younger sisters.

It had been months since they received the terrible news of their parents' traffic accident. The couple had made a trip to the city—a rare event for them—and had never come back. Soon after, Jorani, just twelve years old, dropped out of school to take care of her sisters and her grandmother. It was a load she had never anticipated carrying all on her own, and most days, if she was honest, she stumbled under the weight of the responsibility.

She pulled herself up the steps to the hut and greeted her grandmother, who was slowly folding some laundry. *"Choum reap souar, Yiey."* Her grandmother smiled weakly back at her and stayed focused on her task.

POST CARD

CORRESPONDENCE

Khmer (pronounced K'mai, or Kmy) is the official language of Cambodia. The words in this story are spelled to show the way they might sound in Khmer.

Choum reap souar means "hello."

Ever since she had broken her leg, the older woman had been very frail, and every movement seemed to give her pain. She had been so active and hard-working before, it was hard for Jorani to get used to her being this way.

Their home was small and unremarkable, just a typical wooden frame with walls of woven bamboo. Like others in the area, the hut was raised three meters on stilts, and had a steep thatched roof over-hanging the walls to protect the interior from the heat of the sun and the rain. There were three rooms inside, separated by woven bamboo partitions. The front room was a living room, used for receiving visitors. The room that had been their parents' bedroom

POST CARD

CORRESPONDENCE

Yiey means "Grandmother."

was now for Grandma, and the third room Jorani shared with her sisters.

The girls had followed their big sister into the house, but after a simple breakfast of rice porridge, she sent them out again with little jobs to do. Though the house was small, there was so much to be done to keep things clean and to get meals together every day for the five of them. Jorani sighed as she watched the girls running outside. *How can they really help when they are so small? We need help. Real help. We need food, and medicine for Yiey, and money for school, and clothes, and . . .* She stopped herself. She didn't have time to worry about these things. She needed to come up with a plan.

Jorani watched her grandmother still folding what few towels and sheets they had. *At least she is up now, and doesn't have to sleep so much in the day anymore.* The older one of the girls, Kanya, was nine now, and able to read a little. Jorani thought she could perhaps make a list of tasks for her, enough to keep her busy and to help Yiey. *If they could stay safe*

Many Cambodian villagers live in homes like this one.

for a few hours, I could make it to the market to sell some things.

Jorani went to her room and reached under the mat she shared with her sisters. She pulled out a beautiful woven scarf—it had been her mother's. In it she kept tucked away a small amount of *riel* and U.S. dollars. It was all the money they had. She counted it out and tried to calculate how long it would last, and how much she could spare for the trip to the market. Jorani rubbed her forehead in frustration. She was not at all sure she could make enough money to get the five of them through another month.

She hid the money away again and went to check on a pot of beans she had set to soak last night. Cooking was the easiest of her responsibilities. She had learned a lot from watching her mother and grandmother, and it was fun for her to try to make the same ingredients (beans, rice, noodles) taste differently each time and to use spices that would delight her little sisters. *If only there was enough!*

She arranged the pink flowers she had brought back from the river, placing them in a little jar on the table. Smiling, she stepped back and admired the cozy

POST CARD

CORRESPONDENCE

Riel is the standard unit of Cambodian currency (though U.S. dollars are often used on the streets as well). 1 dollar = 4,000 riel

living room. She tried so hard to make the inside of their dark little hut a bit brighter.

Days of scraping by turned into weeks, and then into two months. Jorani worked as hard as she knew how, making mats to sell at the market, taking care of their few remaining hens so she could sell the eggs, and doing odd jobs such as repairing fishing nets or carrying packages for other villagers, trading her work for food. But still most days her sisters were hungry, and Yiey had long run out of pain medication. Jorani knew she would have to go beyond their village to find work.

This frightened her. She had never been outside of her village. It made her think about her parents and what had happened to them. Where would she go, and how would she get there?

She didn't want to bother her grandmother with these questions—she was so often in pain these days. But Jorani had heard of a neighbor who had helped other girls find jobs in the city waiting tables. Serving people food and drinks—that seemed like something she could do, and an honest way to earn money.

"Choum reap souar?" Jorani called up to the door of the neighbor's hut. She was not sure how many people lived in this house. A tall man with dark eyes came to the door and nodded down at her. "Do you know of a place I could get work? I'm Jorani. I don't know if you know us, but my grandmother was injured in an accident . . ." She felt very nervous all of a sudden. "My parents are passed, and the little girls are not much help . . ." She didn't know what else to say. She didn't mean to sound whiny. Proud even in her poverty, she just wanted to explain why she was asking for help.

The man looked her over for a moment. "Yes, I know of somewhere you can get work. Come back tomorrow at this time, and I will take you there." Then he turned abruptly and went inside.

Somewhere inside Jorani, she felt an alarm go off, but she pushed it away. *Don't be afraid! There isn't anywhere left to go, or anyone else to do it. It's up to you! You can do it!*

Hope does not put us to shame, because God's love has been poured out into our hearts through the Holy Spirit, who has been given to us.

—Romans 5:5

She repeated this mantra to herself as she backed away and ran home.

The next day, when she returned, the neighbor still didn't say much, just motioned for her to follow him. She walked with him for a while until they caught a bus, which took them farther than Jorani had ever traveled. She looked out the dusty window at the sun in the sky, trying to guess how long they had been on the road. *I hope Kanya was able to read my message. I hope the girls are helping Grandmother. I hope I get back tonight before dark. I hope this is a good job and they like me.* Her heart sank as she realized that, since they had come so far, whatever job she got would probably require her to stay nearby during the week while she worked, only going home on weekends, if then.

I hope my hope is enough.

"Who is this?" asked a Khmer man. They had finally reached their destination, a compound in

Phnom Penh

the capital city of Phnom Penh, with high walls and guards at the entrances. Jorani had never seen such a large place. *Maybe I am going to work in his fancy kitchen.* The man looked her over, just like the neighbor had done. He looked at her hands and had her open her mouth. Jorani felt afraid and uncomfortable, and started to tremble a bit.

"Here." He handed the neighbor some money. "She'll be fine. Take this and leave us."

Jorani tried not to show her excitement. She wondered, *If he paid that much just for bringing me here, how much will he pay for my work? This job could save us!* She relaxed for the first time since her journey had begun.

She didn't know what was coming.

Around the time Jorani came into the world, a young Australian man was beginning life with his family. He had a good business, and always thought of himself as a giver, instead of a goer, in relation to God's work in the world. He thought he would make a good living, then give funds to others so they could go serve God wherever he needed them. But questions had begun to take shape in his mind—questions about what he was going to do with his life, and how he could serve . . .

These questions came to a point on a trip to Cambodia. The man saw children living in dumps, with no clothes and no food. Later that day, he felt an urge to do something. As he recalls, he tried to pray for the Defender God to have mercy on these children, but the words that formed in his mind were "God have mercy on me if I don't do something to help these kids."

Eventually, the young family moved to Thailand. There, while doing volunteer work for a mission organization, they heard about a man who had been offered child slaves to do whatever he wanted—he need only pay 400 dollars.

It was then that the man felt God put in his heart a vision to bring an end to child slavery.

After a while, the man who had paid for her grew tired of watching her. He showed her to a room, and left her alone, with no explanation.

Jorani felt something was deeply wrong, but she did not know what to do. *Maybe I can just go.* She wondered if she could find her way home. But she thought that perhaps she just had to wait. She'd come so far, and she didn't know the customs of people in this town. Before she could think much more about it, another man came to the door.

"You have to stay here for one week to train before you can go back home." Then he left and locked the door.

Click. She could not leave.

The week passed. There were long days and longer, terrifying, dark nights. Other girls came and left, and men came too. These men smelled of smoke and something else that made Jorani feel sick, and they hurt Jorani. They hurt the other girls. They did not care who these girls were—what their names were, or how old (or how young) they were. They did not stay to hear the girls cry, or watch them try to tend to their cuts and bruises and other wounds. They just came and left, and locked the door.

Click.

The week of "training" passed, and Jorani felt shame. She had done no good work, and been given no money. And she had been forced to do awful things. Now she felt used up—worthless. She wondered, *If this is training, what's next? And will they ever give me money?* She desperately wanted to go home, but she couldn't go anywhere unless she had something to show for her work.

One day she was speaking with one of the other

girls, telling her story and why she couldn't go home. "The uncles won't be happy that I left my grand-mother alone, and on top of that, I have nothing to show for it." She fought back tears. "I will bring shame on my family."

The other girl told her she had heard there was a place to make easy money, working in restaurants where people came to sing and enjoy music. The place sounded far from the province where Jorani's family lived, but she wanted so much to leave, she almost didn't care where she ended up. At her next chance, she asked her employer about work in Kompong Som.

Jorani planned to escape on this trip and make money somewhere on her own. She thought that any kind of work would be better than what these people had in mind.

Someone in the corner overheard her conversa-tion, and laughed. A female guard spoke up, "If she wants to go to Kompong Som, let me take her."

The guard who transported her to Kompong Som seemed nice enough, but arriving in a new city scared Jorani more than she'd imagined.

> It is estimated that the illegal buying and selling of slaves in Cambodia produces 500 million dollars a year.

The idea of running away suddenly didn't seem all that feasible anymore, and she stuck close to the lady all that day and night. In the morning, the woman took Jorani to a foreign man's house. Immediately upon meeting him, Jorani's skin prickled with fear and her heart raced. Terror curled up in her stomach like river snakes coiled in the sun.

Again, money was exchanged for her delivery. The woman was paid to walk away. And Jorani's heart sank again.

Everyone must have a price.

From one man's vision, an internationally recognized non-profit organization grew. And not just in one country, but in another, and another, and another. Hundreds of employees and volunteers joined together with the goal of rescuing, restoring, protecting, and empowering the fatherless, the motherless, the hopeless . . . the voiceless.

Together they served as hands and feet of their Defender God, to take up the cases of those who could not fight for themselves, of those who had been left wounded. And they were joined by others, teams and agencies and partners in the work.

These are people who have looked in the eyes of enslaved girls and have been convinced that everyone has a price.

And that price has been paid by their Father.

Jorani was shown to her room. A new security guard stood at the end of the hallway. *For a girl who roamed free in a village all day and night, they sure have a lot of guards watching over me. I wonder why they need so many guns? What are they protecting us from?* Then, as her shy smile to the guard was answered with a sneer, something dawned on her.

He's not keeping me safe; he's keeping me prisoner.

There, in the foreign man's house, Jorani became a slave. She was asked to do things she didn't want to do, and was ashamed to do. She worked and wasn't paid. She was hurt, and no one helped her. It didn't matter if she cried, or refused, or got upset. A slave is the property of a master, and this man had paid to be her master. Sometimes in her mind, she would escape—imagining the Mekong or her sisters or her grandmother. Sometimes she remembered the faces of her mother and father. She tried to picture herself in her house,

From Beth's Journal

I recently went to a website where I answered questions about my household and found out how many slaves were used to make the items I enjoy—called my "slavery footprint." It was stunning. We can't pretend this doesn't touch us. It does. It's happening on our watch. But no more. We must speak up and act and give and pray.

or humming a song in the village. It helped. Some.

After a while, this owner also tired of Jorani, and sent her to live in the house of the woman who first brought her there. Sometimes he called for her to come back, and although she never wanted to go, she had no choice. The guards were always watching. They told her they knew where she was from, they knew where her family lived—where her sisters lived. They taunted her and reminded her that she was just a young girl and had no way to fight back. They told her she was worth nothing.

Sometimes, Jorani saw other young girls of different colors and ages at the big house when she was there. Jorani wondered what would happen if they worked together. Could they all break down the

gate? Get past the guards? She longed to gather them around and share her plan, but no one even made eye contact, let alone talked or schemed about escaping.

Jorani later described being escorted out of that house as escaping the tiger's mouth.

In the end, the foreign man paid three million riel in total for her (currently, about seven hundred dollars). The woman told her it was a lot, because she was young and strong. Some slaves were bought and sold for much less.

When the man found Jorani no longer useful, he stopped asking for her. The woman didn't want her either. So, as simple as that, Jorani was turned out to live on the streets, in the province far, far from the village by the river where her sisters and grandmother lived.

Jorani had traveled so far away, yet on the outside, she still looked much like the girl who had left the village that morning long ago. But on the inside, a different journey had been set in motion—one that

took her far from who she used to be.

And she was angry. Anger built up in her like the molten earth forced up into the volcano's mouth—anger at the neighbor who deceived her, anger at the guards who taunted her, anger at the woman who held her hostage, anger at the men who enslaved her. She was angry that her uncles hadn't come to find her, and that she had to leave in the first place. She was angry that her parents had died.

And at the bottom of all that anger, there was fear. *What's going to happen to me? How much longer can I live like this? What use is my life now anyway?*

Back in the village, Jorani's grandmother had been very sick. Weeks of little exercise and pain had made her lungs weak. At the time when Jorani left, she had just taken a turn for the worse, though none of them knew it. The little sisters stayed with her and nursed her. Kanya followed Jorani's instructions, and told no one where her big sister had gone, only that she had found work that would take her from the village for a time.

But the dry season passed, and the wet season came and

went again. Slowly Yiey's health improved. When she realized how long Jorani had been gone, and still heard no word from her, she became very worried.

She reached out to her relatives, and to the other villagers. No one would say where she had gone. Finally one woman whispered to her, "I saw her go with Phirun."

On hearing that name, Jorani's grandmother reached out and steadied herself against the woman's arm. One thought struck her: *My granddaughter is in terrible trouble!*

She quickly scrounged together as much money as she could to take the bus to Phnom Penh. *I lost my daughter here. Will I lose Jorani too?*

In Kompong Som, members of a team of rescue workers were combing the streets, looking for victims of slavery. They went out at night, acting as tourists out on the town just looking to have fun in the restaurants and other places that filled certain dark streets of the city. When they saw girls who looked very young employed at these places, they tried to be friendly with them—they wanted to learn where they were from and who were their employers.

Sometimes the girls would go with them and be taken to safe places where they would be protected from their masters. Sometimes the girls refused to say anything.

They were too afraid.

Finding a job was difficult and Jorani struggled. *I just need to earn enough to get home and have something to offer my family for all this time away.* She wondered how long it would take her to earn enough. And how much was enough? Enough for what?

Jorani's grandmother was struggling too. She felt

According to UNICEF, in the past thirty years, around 30 million children have lost their childhood through slavery. Many people are now working to end this tragedy. Destiny Rescue is a non-profit dedicated to rescuing children from human trafficking. They work in southeast Asia to restore abused children and protect the vulnerable. They, and other groups like them, provide medical care, counseling, financial assistance, education, and often, the only safe place these girls have known.

helpless. How could she ever find such a young girl in a city so big? Still, she pressed on. She came back to the city again, and through lots of questions discovered that Jorani might have been taken to Kompong Som. After some planning and gathering of money, she made the long trip.

Someone, a girl in one of the restaurants she had visited, had pulled her aside and whispered to her the name of a group of people. "They look for lost girls."

With many wrong turns, Jorani's grandmother found the office. She clutched an old photo of Jorani as she opened the door and went inside. Someone greeted her right away and offered her tea. They asked her why she had come. When she had finished telling about her fears and all the details she had learned of the day Jorani left, the staff comforted her. A pleasant young woman made a copy of Jorani's photo and agreed to keep an eye out for her.

"If we hear anything at all, we will call the number you gave us," she promised.

Another six weeks passed.

Then . . . a phone call.

The rescue worker wasn't sure. The face looked so different, and her hair was pulled back. But the eyes. The eyes looked like those that had stared out of that photo at her, hanging there on her wall in the office for all these weeks.

She thought of just calling out the girl's name to see if she turned her head, but she didn't want to frighten her. So instead she waited, hovering around the entrance to the karaoke place, looking for an opportunity.

"I *love* your scarf! Can I buy one like that here?" the rescue worker asked the girl.

The girl's hand went nervously to her throat—but her face stayed smiling. "No, it came from a village market." The name of the village slipped out before the girl realized what she'd said. "It was my mother's." It was clear she didn't suspect this foreign woman was anything but a tourist.

It's now or never, the worker thought, checking to see where the guards were. "I'm Dana," she said. "What's your name?"

Within the week, the grandmother had borrowed, begged, and scraped enough money to travel once again.

She first saw her from the back. Tears sprang to her eyes.

Jorani.

"Yiey, I can't come with you." Jorani was full of emotions. Happy to see her grandmother walking around, happy to see her at all. Sad to be found here, looking like this, all made up and dressed to draw attention. She begged her grandmother not to tell her

sisters where she was. "I have nothing to offer the family; I am not a good example for my sisters anymore, and I have nothing to show for my time away.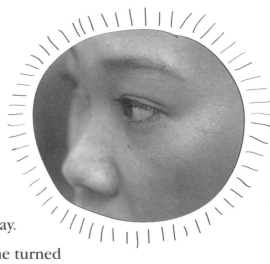
It would be disgraceful." She turned her face away and looked around nervously, expecting a guard to catch her and take her back. "You are better off leaving me here. Just make something up."

The grandmother tried all day to change her mind, but Jorani stood firm.

She cried herself to sleep that night.

Her grandmother didn't sleep well that night either. But she had thought of a plan. In the morning, she went back to Jorani and told her the family was having a Buddhist ceremony that she couldn't miss. It would be a dishonor of the highest form. "After the ceremony days," she assured her, "if you still want to, you can return to the city."

The rescue workers at the office that had helped the grandmother also arranged the transportation for Jorani to get out of the city. On the way to the village, one of the workers gently explained to Jorani that there was a third option. Jorani didn't have to stay in the city, and she didn't have to go home.

The staff of this rescue group had created a home for girls like Jorani—girls who had been mistreated and made to feel ashamed. Girls who had no place to go, no money to get them out of their situations, and not enough education to make them confident in their own talents and skills. It was a safe place—a place of healing and growth.

Jorani listened intently as the woman described the home. But when the woman said there were girls there just like Jorani, she shook her head sadly.

"Like me? I don't think so."

"Exactly like you . . ." the rescuer replied, tilting her head and looking directly into Jorani's dark eyes.

Jorani glanced at her grandmother, who nodded back at her and took her hand.

"*Jaa,*" Jorani whispered, "*k'Nyum nung Dthul.*"

When they arrived at this home for girls, the grandmother listened as the counselor explained how Jorani would receive regular counseling, schooling, and vocational training. She could be there for as many years as she needed, until she felt like she could return to her village with something to show for her years away.

Tears started to fall down Jorani's cheeks. "Yiey, I am so sorry." Her shoulders shook with sobs, "Thank you for coming to look for me. Thank you for not giving up. One day I will come back . . ."

After her grandmother left, Jorani settled into

POST CARD

Jaa, k'Nyum nung Dthul means "Yes, I will go."

her new home. In the next few weeks, the first step for Jorani was to remember the dreams she had once held as a child. The counselors talked to her about her future and creating a vision for it, so she had something to work toward. That part came easy— right before she left, she had a dream of caring for her grandmother, of helping to make a home for her sisters, of being a provider.

"I am creative," she admitted, when pressed. "Maybe . . . I could learn sewing skills so I could open a tailor shop and become a dressmaker in my village."

Her counselor nodded encouragingly, and Jorani smiled.

A dream was taking shape.

One of the obstacles for Jorani in her healing was her negative feelings about herself. Since she had been raised as a Buddhist, she was heavily influenced by beliefs of a person's value coming from having right thoughts and right goals, right words and right deeds. Jorani feared that her life had been tainted— that because she had not had right thoughts and views and actions, she no longer had hope for being released from suffering, for finding true peace and happiness. She had no hope of experiencing a pure mind and heart.

Her only hope was that, by working hard at sewing and earning enough money, she could care for her grandmother and earn her way back on the path of enlightenment—the Buddhist way. One day during class, she acknowledged this goal. "I hope I can do good work that will make up for the years I lost."

The sewing instructor stopped the class and looked at Jorani, "What do you mean? Why do you need to make up for those years?"

"To show respect for Buddha . . . for my family, for my next life," she answered. "I hope one day I am good enough to erase all the hard things that have happened to me."

The instructor came over to Jorani and said, "May I tell you a story?" Jorani nodded and put her project down.

"There is a big, epic story I wonder if you have ever heard?" the instructor began. "It starts with a God who created all that you see . . . the river, the trees, the rice we will eat today at lunch. He even created you! But God has an enemy, someone who opposes his work here on earth. That enemy tricked the first man and woman into sin—doing wrong—and that sin has separated us from God ever since."

By now the other girls had stopped their sewing too. The instructor's words caught their attention.

They knew all about enemies and being tricked.

"But God made a way for that separation to be bridged—a way for his creation, for men and women, to be close to him again, to know his love and his peace. He sent his pure Son from Heaven to die on a cross, for your sins and for mine. That was how much he paid to get us back—to get you back. He gave his

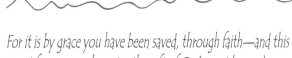

For it is by grace you have been saved, through faith—and this is not from yourselves, it is the gift of God—not by works, so that no one can boast.

—Ephesians 2:8, 9

Son for you." Jorani's eyes opened wide. Why would God pay so much for her?

The instructor went on. "Only God could erase this sin, and so, because God himself paid the price for sin, it's no longer held against his children, the ones who believe in him. God paid this price because he loves you so much. In fact, he loves us so much, he wants us to live with him forever in Heaven, where there is no pain, and no suffering."

One of the girls asked, "But we must have to do something to get this love, yes?"

The instructor looked at each of the girls. "He wants to be your Father. A good and perfect Father. He doesn't love you because of what you do or don't do, or what you have done or not done. He loves you because he created you." She let that sink in with them a moment. "He is a good Father, and he is a strong Father. He will defend you. He showed both his love for us and his power when his Son died on the cross. Because he didn't stay dead! Three days after he died, Jesus, God's Son, rose again and lived! He showed that God could defeat any enemy, even Death."

Jorani's heart began to beat faster. She wanted to know this God. Did he know her? Did he want to defend her? Is it possible she didn't have to *do* everything right to serve him, to know his peace? She had trouble understanding a God who did not require anything of her—who only wanted to love her, and for her to love him.

Her thoughts were broken into by the voice of her teacher. "In the Bible, God's Word, you can read his story. The enemy designed a plan to steal and kill and destroy, but God will use all of your experiences, all of the suffering you have gone through, to create in you compassion toward others, and a reliance on him. Jesus says in the Bible, 'I came so [you] can have real and eternal life, more and better life than [you] ever dreamed of'" (John 10:10, *The Message*).

One of the most amazing and loving ways God the Defender protects us is through saving us from ourselves. He saves us from our anger, from self-hatred and fear, from hurts we hold in our hearts, and memories that threaten to stop our growing, stretching, and serving. The apostle Paul was a prisoner more than once—he knew about being hurt and mistreated. He wrote, "We have this treasure in jars of clay to show that this all-surpassing power is from God and not from us. We are hard pressed on every side, but not crushed; perplexed, but not in despair; persecuted, but not abandoned; struck down, but not destroyed" (2 Corinthians 4:7-9). Paul was a man who knew his Defender and spent every day learning how to serve him better. Will you try with me to do the same?

Better life than I ever dreamed of? For me?

"God wants a relationship with you. He wants you to know that, even when you were doing wrong, even when bad things were being done to you, he loved you and planned for you to be with him. He wants you to believe in your heart that what his Son did on the cross changes everything. And he wants you to commit to getting to know him, and learning to love him."

Jorani knew that this God was speaking to her heart. She jumped up and said to the teacher, "Jaa! I want to know this God—the One who defends me and loves me and planned for me. I want to know him."

Jorani spent a happy and healing time at the rescue home. She loved taking care of those around her, especially the younger children. And her housemothers loved having her there because of her servant's heart and her bright personality. With time and lots of care, Jorani began to shine like her name, which means "radiant jewel."

At the end of that year, Jorani safely returned to village life. She was given a sewing machine and all the equipment and training to start her own small sewing business. Today, she is reaching for her dream of operating her own business and providing for her family. "I know God has a plan for me," she says.

And we can't wait to see it unfold . . .

In our modern world, it's hard to imagine people living as slaves today. But there are millions who are forced into slavery through poverty, lack of education, and lack of hope. How can you make a stand against slavery and serve as a defender of children around the world who are being enslaved?

Many people are not in physical prisons, but are made slaves to sin, slaves to self-pity, and slaves to their situation, whatever that may be. First Peter 2:16 says "Live as free people, but do not use your freedom as a cover-up for evil; live as God's slaves." What do you think it means to be God's slave? What is the best way to find and hold on to freedom?

Write your thoughts about Jorani's story here.

Chapter 5

THE PAGES AFTER

I was speaking this year at an event called the Champions of Faith, an awards ceremony for people who had remarkably contributed to some area of Christian service. There were honorees who were authors, in Christian music, in business, in missions, etc. I was coming straight from Haiti—in fact, I got off the plane and didn't even have time to shower! But I knew what I was going to say, and when it was time, I stepped onto the stage.

Then I saw her: Vonette Bright.

She was being honored that night with a lifetime achievement award for her part in founding the organization Campus Crusade for Christ (now "Cru") with her husband, the late Bill Bright. More than sixty years ago, they decided to start an organization for students that taught them to reach out on their college campuses and around the world to those who didn't know Jesus. Now Cru is international and has touched tens of millions of people. She rightly deserved to be honored.

It was in 1993 that my now husband and I went to Albania, a country on the other side of the world, with that same organization. While we were there, we visited an orphanage. It stirred something in us that years later would be in part what caused us to start the international branch of Back2Back Ministries, aimed specifically at serving international orphans.

When I saw her, now in her eighties, sitting in the front row, I changed my plan and tossed aside my notes. I looked right down at her and started: "We have a Storyweaver. He uses our stories and our obedience in those stories in ways we can't even imagine. Mrs. Bright, I pledged my heart to the nations almost twenty years ago, while on a trip with the organization you started, and although we have never met, your life has had a profound impact on mine." I continued on with tears in my eyes, "Your decision to follow the plan God had for you touched me, and now is touching orphans you won't meet until we are all on the other side of eternity. Thank you for trusting him enough to follow a story of his making."

The Storyweaver is always at work. He moves long before we even know our need and uses our story lines generations later. Each of the stories you hold now in your hand started long before the events I recorded here. Yours and mine did, too! I had great-grandparents who were both pastors and supporters of missions. They raised my grandmother and her brothers to be in ministry, and our reunions were always full of hymn singing and people asking each other, "How's it going with your soul?" All of that played a part in my serving as a missionary.

Sometimes God uses the good in our stories to prompt us to do more good, and sometimes he uses the hard, to show us there is another path. Either way, we can be confident "in all things God works for the good of those who love him" (Romans 8:28). One of the hard parts of my story is I lost my dad to cancer. This loss is not necessarily any easier today than it was when it happened, but I have seen God use it as I talk to fatherless children around the world. It's just one example of how he uses all of our story, all of the time.

And there are so many story lines happening at once! I have story lines as a writer, wife, mother, missionary, friend, sister, daughter, aunt, and the list goes on and on.

You have lots of story lines going on as well, story lines at school or at co-op, story lines in your family, in your neighborhood, in your church, on your sports teams or in your music groups. God is also weaving you into the lives of children around the world, with each prayer you utter and each dollar you share!

There aren't just story lines we can see today, but story lines from the past that brought your parents together, that brought you to the town you are in, or to the school you attend. There are story lines in the future—people and places you will visit and be called to serve or share with. With all of that epic storytelling going on, it's a good thing there is a Storyweaver we can trust to keep it all straight!

Just take a closer look at some of the story lines of the people you met in this book.

The people who gave Jorani a home during her healing and restoration from slavery were from a group founded in 2001, back when Jorani was still living happily with her parents as a little girl. God saw her need ahead and stirred his people to action in preparation for Jorani's story and many others like her. Lots of relationships went into her rescue and restoration. Read the following real-life letter she wrote to her sponsor who helped pay her expenses while she was learning about sewing . . . and Jesus:

How is your family? I am very well. I was very, very happy on Christmas day. I know that your family was also happy on Christmas day. I am going back home in January 2012. I am very excited when I knew that I am going back home soon.

The reasons that I am very happy to go back home are:

- First: I can look after my grandmother.
- Second: I can open my small sewing business.
- Third: I am very very happy because I can help my family.

I want to say thank you for you to be my sponsors. Thank you so much for your love. I love your family so much and I am going to remember all of your love that have given to me.

Jorani doesn't know what her future holds, but she knows God has a plan for her.

We can stay a part of her story line and other rescued slaves by praying for their re-entry into their families or villages, for their health and the healing of their memories. We can pray they can grow and develop a healthy family. Most important, we can pray they understand their Defender God loves them deeply.

I have a God-story in my own family that made me eager to share Joseph and Ben's. It was in 1997 that I first heard the beat of my adopted son's heart in my own. I didn't know his name, I didn't know how old he would be or when he would come, but much like a mother can feel a baby kick, I felt him kick in my heart. He was real to me, and I wanted to meet him.

Evan came into our family as a baby the next year and is now in high school. His story line blending with mine is one of the greatest blessings God has ever given me! I love how God knew that although Evan was born in another country, he was always intended to be my son. As anybody who has gone through an adoption will tell you, there are too many

A young *Emma* and *Evan* enjoy a *picnic*.

details that have to come together for there not to be a Storyweaver orchestrating it all!

Ben and Joseph's parents had to find themselves at the same place in the same time, fall in love, get married, have a heart for adoption, then Ethiopia, then not just for one, but for two—and all at the exact time Ben and Joseph, in separate stories, were released for adoption.

Whew! All of that doesn't just happen! And though we may read about them and think God wrote that story just for their family now, I'm sure their story will go on to impact Ben's future grandsons and Joseph's future neighbors or employees. God brought them here to set off events we can't even imagine yet! He knew he wanted those stories told in this setting, so he took the hard and used it for his good.

That's God's way. He can't help but redeem and repair and reconcile and restore and rescue. It's his Defender nature.

We all have things that make life challenging for us. In Antonio's case, some of those things are obvious when you meet him; for many others, those things are hidden. We might be shy, or struggle taking tests, or feel anxiety for no reason; we might have trouble reading, or have severe allergies. None of us is struggle-free. One of the reasons Antonio's life touches everyone around him (and everyone who reads or hears his story) is that he reminds us that each person, in God's eyes, is deeply valuable.

It's why I love the Bible story of Mephibosheth, a young disabled boy who was the son of Jonathan and the grandson of King Saul. After his father died, he was forgotten and left behind. But he, like Antonio, was rescued, and was given a new family, and a place always at the king's table. Our Defender-Kinsman defends the value of all people and gives us way more than what others think we are worth, and certainly more than we deserve. We can follow his example and do the same!

I can't wait to see what God is going to do through Antonio, but it's not to be measured by human standards. He doesn't ever have to do something great for us to say, "Ahh . . . now I understand why he was spared." He was spared simply because God loves him as his son and has stories still to be told through him on earth. Once those stories are over, God will bring him home. Antonio can't earn that kind of love and doesn't deserve it. None of us does—and that's the miracle.

Caitlyn's story moved me while I was writing it, because I could picture her, sitting in her room, listening to the chaos around her, wondering if there was a God and if there was, did he even notice her? Meanwhile, unbeknownst to her, God was moving in Sheryl's heart, walking her family through a path to prepare them for Caitlyn's story line. He not only saw her, he was coming to her rescue!

Psalm 68:6 says, "God places the lonely in families" (*NLT*). This family is a living testimony to that truth! And to think, God used Sheryl's past, the other foster children that had been in her home, a relationship from church, a couple of big brothers—all of it to accomplish his purpose. Once again, that is an awful lot of storyweaving!

There are children like Caitlyn and her brother Cameron all over the U.S. Almost half a million children live in foster families, or group homes, right in our communities. They are all around us and we don't have to travel anywhere to begin to bring them into our story lines. How might you be able to pray for them, share with them, or include them in your church or small group? What kinds of things do they need physically, emotionally, socially, spiritually, or educationally? And what do you have to offer them? These are all great questions for you to talk about with your parents or church leader.

And if you are a foster kid now, this message is for you too! There is a God who loves you and wants to be your Father. There are people who want to help you be all that he created you to be. Find those people and hang on to them. Tell them your worries. Tell them your ideas. And ask them to be your partner in helping other kids in your own country . . . and beyond!

One of our U.S.-based staff members, Chris Cox, shared with me the following story, about an American girl like Caitlyn:

In a small church in Peebles, Ohio, a woman was given a vision from God to start a soup kitchen. After a miraculous launch to this ministry, a local children's home asked this woman for help from her soup kitchen. She connected them to her church and her church offered scholarships to children from the home for one week of church camp. Tina was one of three girls from the children's home sent to camp.

When she arrived at the event, she wanted to go home immediately. She kept saying, "This isn't for me . . . it's just too much, too big." Her leaders coached her into staying the first night. On Monday she still wanted to go home, so I (Chris) met with her. As I do with any student who wants to go home, I asked her to trust me for twenty-four hours, and if she hated it by dinner on Tuesday, I would recommend that the directors of the home come and pick her up. That night the message spoke to Tina. She heard God speaking into her heart, telling her that her past didn't define her value. She went to bed that night with more peace than she had experienced in a long time.

On Tuesday morning her first experience was a Justice Station, set up with 200 pictures of Back2Back orphan kids that students could pray over. She was invited to write a letter to the B2B kids, telling them how God had revealed himself in her life. Tina wrote to Busheera, a child in India, of how she was an orphan too, how she had been abused by her dad and stepdad. She told her of her drug use, attempted suicide, and then her reconciliation to God.

In her own words, "I promise you that everything you're going through now is only gonna make you a better and stronger person. . . . You're never alone, so when you're down or need someone to talk to, you can write me or just talk to the man who gave his life for us, so we wouldn't have to."

The Storyweaver wove the soup kitchen lady into the life of the church, into the life of the children's home, into the life of Tina, into the life of Chris and her leaders, into the life of Busheera, and now into our lives, and ultimately into life with him!

Tina's letter.

I am grateful I see life as a story, and I hope you are too! It helps me when I wake up to decide what to do. I ask myself, "What makes a better story?" When things get hard (and they do and they will), I remind myself there are more chapters to come—and the best stories have conflict.

God is using you! And will continue to do so, if you just say yes. That's my goal, to say yes every morning to whatever he brings me. Yes to praying for someone else, when it's easier to just list my own needs. Yes to giving money or things or time or myself, when I don't always feel like it. Yes to going across the street and greeting someone I don't even know, and think I don't have time for. Yes to serving him, even if it requires getting dirty or getting sick or getting into situations where I have no control.

Yes to being a part of the work of the Defender God.

Beth wrote her first book in third grade. It was about a frog. Mrs. Pate may never have liked it, but her mother still takes it out and looks at it occasionally. Since then, Beth has written other books, such as *Reckless Faith* (Zondervan, 2008), *Relentless Hope* (Standard Publishing, 2011), and *Tales of the Not Forgotten* (Standard Publishing, 2012).

Beth has a houseful of kids—there are some in elementary, a couple in junior high, a high-schooler, a few college students, and two who live independently now. Besides her family, Beth likes all forms of chocolate, the ocean in any season, traveling, and Christmastime.

Beth met her husband, Todd, at age seventeen at Young Life Bible study. She knew she liked him when he offered her one of his three versions of the Bible (since she had forgotten hers). Together they live in Monterrey, Mexico, where they invite you and your family to visit anytime.

ABOUT BEN AND JOSEPH

You read about Ben and Joseph in Chapter 1. But they were kind enough to let us ask them a few more questions about their amazing story. If you have more questions for Ben and Joseph, or about any of the other stories in this book, ask your parents for permission to send your questions and comments to Beth Guckenberger at beth@bethguckenberger.com. She would love to hear from you!

Ben and Joseph, we know you were very young when you first met your adoptive mom and dad. How did you find out you were adopted?

Joseph: When I was two years old, my mom and dad told me that they adopted me and told me the story. I sometimes remember small things about Ethiopia.

BEN: My family talked to me about it. They showed me pictures of when we were in Ethiopia.

What do you know about your home country?

JOSEPH: That it is a beautiful country. It is full of people that live in poverty. I also know that many children there do not get to attend school and learn. I love injera, which is a type of Ethiopian bread.

BEN: I know that they speak a different language from what we speak in America. They speak Amharic. I know that people in Ethiopia look like me; they have brown skin.

What do you like to do? What's your favorite thing to do for fun?

JOSEPH: My favorite sport is football. I am playing flag football this year. I like reading about space, science, football, the periodic table, chemistry, and anatomy. I also like riding my Ripstik.

BEN: I like to create different things. I can make a project out of anything! I also like to color and draw. I also like playing Legos with my brother when I get home from school.

What do you like best about your family?

JOSEPH: What I like best about my family is that they love me. I also like that they take good care of me.

BEN: I love having brothers and a sister to play with. I like going out and being together with my family.

What is something that is a challenge for you?

JOSEPH: Something that is a challenge for me is to control my temper.

BEN: It is hard for me to be neat and organized.

How do you think God is our Defender?

JOSEPH: I think that he defends us by putting a shield of love and angels around our family to keep us safe. He is always protecting us.

BEN: He blocks anything bad that comes our way. He has our backs. He helps us in making the right choices.

What do you think you want to be when you grow up?

JOSEPH: I want to be a scientist. I would like to make cures for diseases.

BEN: When I grow up, I would like to invent toys.

What do you want people to know about or learn from your story in this book?

JOSEPH: Because I know that a lot of children don't have homes, I hope that this would help people make that choice to adopt.

BEN: *I want them to learn about God. I want them to learn that God can help us and take care of us.*

Do you have a favorite Bible verse? If so, what is it, and why do you like it?

JOSEPH: *John 3:16, because it says that God loves us. Every time I think about it, I feel peace inside of me.*

BEN: My favorite part of the Bible is when Jesus gave his life for us. This is my favorite because I am thankful that Jesus gave his life for me so that I can live with God forever.

Acknowledgments

A book takes many cheerleaders. Here is a list of my line-up.

Thank you to all the folks at Standard: Laura, Lindsay, Dale, Bob, Stephanie, Mark, Lu Ann, Ruth, Matt and all of the design and production team. You all have championed this book and more importantly, the idea that children can engage in missions wherever they are. Thank you for sharing these stories on your platform.

Thank you, Back2Back Ministries staff, for working day in and day out in multiple countries to defend the children God has introduced you to. I count you as my closest friends.

Thank you Destiny Rescue, the Walatka family, Rick Norquist, and the foster family represented in this book for sharing your stories with children everywhere. I pray they bring God glory and move his children to action!

Thank you sweet family, for so much more than I can capture in this paragraph. Thank you for loving our crazy life, for listening to pages I have written, for carrying boxes of books in and out of churches and cars, for being your amazing and flexible selves, for listening to me go on and on about something I just heard or wrote or saw . . . and lastly, for loving the children God brings into our life. I trust the Storyweaver with you.

Thank you, Todd, for being supportive and all that means between you and me. I am in awe of how God has led us.

And Jesus, thank you for writing my story. I love waking up each day anticipating what the next page will say.

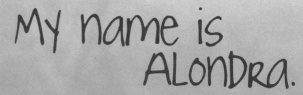

My name is ALONDRA.

I love to swim and listen to music. I like math and want to be a teacher when I grow up.

Alondra is a confident eight-year-old, full of laughter and curiosity. Her favorite color is purple, she has two siblings, and she has lived in an orphanage for as long as she can remember. Each morning, she wakes up in a dormitory full of other girls and walks to school. In the evening, she does her homework and chores before going to bed.

Alondra is just one of 163 million orphaned children in our world. But unlike many other orphans, Alondra will wake up tomorrow knowing she's loved by her Father God. She will see God's love through her good meals, through her tutor after school, through her houseparents who care for her daily, through the visiting families who come to play with her, and through the Back2Back staff who hold her hand at church. Alondra may be physically orphaned, but she is wonderfully loved.

want to learn how to make a difference?

Ask your parents to help you learn more about the orphans Beth Guckenberger and her team serve by visiting www.back2back.org.

Back2Back Ministries • 513.754.0300 • P.O. Box 70, Mason, OH 45040

My name is Daniel.

I like to play soccer and climb the rocks behind my house. My favorite subject is English.

Daniel lives in Jos, Nigeria, where he attends Back2Back's Education Center. At the center, he has good meals, care when he is sick, and a safe place to learn.

When Daniel first came to the Education Center, he was very shy. He rarely laughed or smiled. But now, through the love and attention of Back2Back staff, he has grown to become a confident boy, full of laughter and joy.

Daniel hopes to be a teacher when he grows up. For the first time in his life, Daniel is thriving and well on his way to reaching his goals for a brighter tomorrow.

want to learn how to make a difference?

Ask your parents to help you learn more about the orphans Beth Guckenberger and her team serve by visiting www.back2back.org.

Back2Back Ministries • 513.754.0300 • P.O. Box 70, Mason, OH 45040

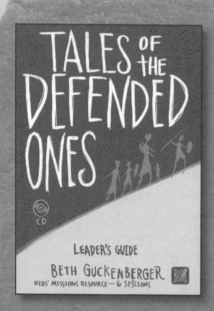